900 Miles

E.J. Runyon

Published by Inspired Quill: March 2020
First Edition

TW: This book contains mentions of drug abuse and suicide.

Chief Editor: Sara-Jayne Slack
Cover Design: Vince Haig: barquing.com
Typeset in Adobe Garamond Pro

Paperback ISBN: [978-1-908600-93-6]
eBook ISBN: [978-1-908600-94-3]
Print Edition

Printed in the United Kingdom
1 2 3 4 5 6 7 8 9 10

Inspired Quill Publishing, UK
Business Reg. No. 7592847
www.inspired-quill.com

Praise for E.J. Runyon

Runyon tells her stories with an unashamed truthfulness. The work is edgy, but never gratuitously so, never for the sake of edginess. At the same time, there exists a compelling emotional accessibility. If you are willing to risk reading, it will challenge you, capture your attention, and dare you to continue till the very last.

—Catherine Ryan Hyde,
author of *Pay it Forward*

With this collection, Runyon is following in the tradition of the great regional American writers. Flannery O'Connor, John Fante, Bret Harte, and Sinclair Lewis. The triumph of their stories was due in part to the writers' craftsmanship and vision, but also to the honesty of the narrative which grounded the fictive worlds deeply in reality.

—Adam Burgess,
author and owner of *Roof Beam Reader*

[This novel] is an original, powerful, and well-written book that we highly recommend.

—*LOTL Magazine*

It is a wonderfully told story, and utterly compelling. Not only is the writing outstanding, but the core essence of the story is well worth pondering as it carries its painful realities to a completely satisfying resolution. I urge you to read and savor this exceptional book. You'll be glad you did.

—Lloyd A. Meeker,
Out in Print

*For NCG
and all the miles we drove in the late of our evenings.*

Chapter One

THE SCALE READS 185.

"Cool." Christina nods, her damp hand against the wall to steady herself, bath towel pressed tight to her middle so she could see the jiggling numbers. "Eighteen and five. Cool. Just three more to find and I'm a rich girl." She steps off the scale and sets her leg up on the rim of the tub to squirt pale yellow lotion along the length of her shin.

Her towel drops away and the remaining patches of dampness tingle on the back of her thighs and neck, giving her goosebumps. "Maybe twenty again?" She wouldn't be twenty-one for another nine months. Twenty is a valid number. No? "Sure. Five, eighteen, and twenty."

She tries saying the numbers aloud but the leaning over and rubbing with the lotion takes her breath away, so she straightens up.

Fingertips pressing at her sternum, her inhale whistling though her mouth; air-drying while considering the last two numbers. Christina waits then exhales, pondering whether she should bother cutting her toenails too. She goes easier with lotioning the other leg, leaning to the left and only using one hand, that way she wasn't pressing her ribs up against her thigh.

Nicky walks into the bathroom and stands, staring. She feels his eyes on her behind, what the view must be like from back there. Ignores him until he rubs his head against her already lotioned leg and meows, low and hungry. "Okay, just a minute, big boy. Mama's busy." Two more to find. Two more. And maybe 19 was better than 20. She thinks about it... *five, eighteen, and nineteen. Yeah. nineteen.*

Harrison sits at the table, drinking his morning pot of coffee. His empty bong at his elbow, and the usual murk of sweet smoke wreathing his head and shoulders. From as far back as Christina could remember, way back when she was small, even when her mother was still there with them, Harrison's morning ritual started this way. Three bowls in the bong and a full pot of coffee just for him; that was breakfast.

He blamed it on being a lineman for the phone company: "Up this pole in the wind and rain, down that smelly vault all fricken' summer, all kinds of crummy weather; hell of a life."

Years had passed. Her mother kicked it in a pretty ugly way. The trees out front and Christina herself grew taller; both of them passing up Harrison's 5'6". But Harrison's song remained the same.

She pulls a chocolate-chip muffin and a can of cat food from the fridge. "Hey, gimme a number."

"God, it's Wednesday, isn't it?"

She sets the can down for Nicky. "I need two more. Got anything?"

Harrison sips, staring down at the big Maine Coon's fluffy rear-end, considering. Christina waits. Peels the paper off her muffin, careful with any fugitive chips, but he shakes his head. "Nope. I'm blank, baby."

"Okay." She touches the top of his head and reaches for her house key and bus pass from the bowl on the counter. "I'll leave your dinner in the fridge."

They live on West Heil Avenue, west of Imperial. In El Centro, California. One of the newest and poorest of all of California's fifty-eight counties. Bordering both Arizona and Mexico. The zipper tongue on the open jacket. *Birthplace of Cher,* Christina thinks whenever she sees a state map.

Because of the house's southern exposure on its rear side and before the trees had gotten big enough to shade the kitchen window, her mom took to calling it Hell Avenue. Back when they first moved in. The family there only seven months before that day in January. Rain; red-light runner.

The walk to the bus is a short one. She only minds it during the summers. And the winters. And it's the beginning of February now. She doesn't drive. Doesn't want to see Harrison's stricken face if she ever climbs behind the wheel of something.

At the newspaper, the El Centro Outlook, *the Outrage* as the employees thought of it, Christina spends part of each morning taking ads over the phone and, on rare occasions, from those who bother walking in. She's also responsible for proofing the ads that come in through the new website, before sending them on for copy setting. The rest of her morning, she files the Account Receivables from last week, and apologizes with her eyes every time someone gripes about having to come to her for the key to the supply cabinet.

Today the dryness of the papers that she shoves into the tight file drawers rubs her bitten cuticles raw, and so she hisses a lot between shaking and blowing on her fingertips; which leave pale trails of bright red on all the file folders.

In between customers at the counter, she tries coming up with her last two numbers. "Gina, gimme a number, I only need two more."

"You gonna give me a fifth a' what you win?"

"Yeah, right." The two girls go through this dance every week Christina buys a ticket. It's part of the purchase now. She wouldn't feel right skipping it.

"Then figure out your own damn numbers." Gina grins, turning back to her stack of payables.

Just before their 10 o'clock break Gina walks her blue ledger printout over to Christina's desk, and sets it down, pointing to the last line posted. She taps her long orange fingernail at the final amount listed in the column: $27.27. "There you go, dearie, twenty-seven. How's that for a winner, huh?"

"I'll take it." Christina stands and stretches. "No charge?"

"You win with this; you owe me a lunch. A full on, hour an' a half, call in and lie to The Beast, my choice of food—Margaritas included—no arguments, celebratory lunch."

"You got a deal."

Finding her last number was a fluke.

A tall guy waited at the Ads counter when morning break ended, Native American looking, hair parted down the middle and falling below his earlobes. Bleached chambray shirt with a little rip fraying the collar; his once-black jeans heading toward a charcoal grey. He tapped his pink Ad card against the counter and smiled. Christina took it and read it back to him out loud; standard procedure.

"Harold Two Threes?" She narrowed her eyes, looked up. The guy grinned. His teeth were very white.

"Harold Two Trees."

She stopped noticing his teeth. Hid her grin. *2-3*. She returned her attention to his card. Baby furniture for sale. She took his payment for a two-week run and smiled like her teeth were just as shiny.

He told her, "You've got the biggest smile." And added, "Thanks." Touching the rim of his hat.

She handed over his change, told him, "No, thank *you*." Really meaning it as she watched him dip his chin and pocket his receipt.

"Whoa." Gina said when Christina hurried over to her desk and whispered about Mr. Two Trees and his number. "You owe me a lunch, Baby Doll. I feel it in my bones."

By noon, Christina has them all: 5, 18, 19, 23, and 27. During her lunch break an hour later, there are four other folks in line buying tickets, two in front of her, two behind. Matt at the 7-Eleven prints out her ticket, holding it to his forehead, not quite squinting, as he predicts, "Yep. This's a good one, here. Big bucks for sure." But then something like that comes out of his mouth every week, and the squinting is just a ploy for some discreet staring at her chest, like she can't tell that. Skinny fool.

"If it makes it, I'll buy you a carton of Marlboros."

"Camels." Matt winks, handing her the ticket. "If it makes it, buy me a case." The girl behind her shifts. Sighs. None too subtle.

"We'll see. Thanks." And the irritated girl moves forward, squeezing past Christina's elbow, and hands Matt the numbers she's chosen.

Now Christina stands back out on the sidewalk, sending up a prayer that this one would make it, so she'd never have to be sure to get back from lunch to the Outrage by 1:45. Never have to deal with all those little pink 6 x 4 cards with the bad handwriting, and the tight A/R file drawers. Never have to wait through Matt's squinting either, ever again.

Christina stops for dinner stuff at the Safeway. She's been cooking for Harrison since she was eleven and her mom bought her a Better Homes and Gardens Step-By-Step Kids Cookbook. They spent days deciding on a special menu for his twenty-seventh birthday. Her mom showed her the trick of staggering the starting times of the courses to make everything come out warm and ready at the same time.

"Well look at this!" Harrison kept saying with each new spoonful she proudly heaped on his plate. She remembered how his ironed shirt smelled of fabric softener as he leaned toward her at the table, whispering just to her, 'Is it our anniversary?' eyebrows raised. The cranberry juice in tall plastic wine glasses, cobalt blue. Her mom's favorite color.

Four months later Harrison was burning dinners left and right, when they remembered to eat, until she stepped up and began risking things from the cookbook to try on her own. She started picking at her cuticles then, too, the same way her mom always did. Christina felt it allowed her to hold onto her in some little way…

She runs her Debit card and selects cash back $7.00. The cashier asks, "No coupons today?"

In the kitchen, Nicky waits, studious about staring intently at the floor, in case food magically appears. It could happen. Christina makes sure it does. She sets Harrison's wrapped plate of *arroz con pollo*, with peas on the side, in the refrigerator. Cleans up the frying pan and the spatula before she sits down to her own heaped plate. The radio plays some old singer, some ballad Harrison would know all the words to. Christina usually eats alone. Every day he said he would, but Harrison never came directly home. When she was in high school it felt great and she could bring her homework to the kitchen table. But now, without homework, eating alone kind of sucked.

I gotta meet some new people, she thinks. She pushes a piece of chicken off her plate and over the edge of the table. It bounces and she watches Nicky pounce. She rubs her eyes, asks Nicky, "So, what's on the agenda tonight, Big Boy?"

It takes her under 10 minutes to finish dinner.

She's cleaned the kitchen. Dinner sits waiting for Harrison, if he drags his skinniness home from wherever he is. Now, there was just the half hour till they pulled the numbers. She could drink a soda from the fridge or walk to the corner and get a Big Gulp before the show. Chips might be nice. *Yeah. That sounds good.*

At 7 o'clock Nicky meows and crawls up next to Christina's lap, pushing his wide head under her hand for a scratch. She sits with her Lotto ticket and takes pink lemonade sips from her plastic Big Gulp cup. Tapping the cup's side, waiting to hear the numbers. A bag of chips leans against her thigh. Cool Ranch. Consolation, in case. She'd eaten the two York Peppermint Patties walking home from the corner store.

The commercial ends and as the familiar music rises up, her shoulders round, she sets her elbows on her knees, chanting her numbers: *5-18-19-23-27. 5-18-19-23-27. 5-18-19-23-27,* till she realizes she can't breathe that way and sits back against the sofa, feet up on the coffee table, jeans unbuttoned.

The first one they call is Gina's number: *27. Good co-worker*, Christina thinks, *I owe you.* One down.

Then comes the 18. She takes another sip anc pushes the bangs off her forehead. *If I win, I'm cutting my hair off, all of it and I'm never wearing it long again.*

Then they read off the five. *Oh my God. Three of 'em!*

Chapter Two

CHRISTINA'S FINGERTIP GOES to her mouth; she bites down hard against the quick and tastes the reassurance of blood. *C'mon, 19. C'mon, 23.* She thinks about being skinny enough to wear linen shorts and tanks and clunky sandals just like the stuff in The Territory Ahead catalogs that come in the mail. Of planting a big spreading tree in the back yard for Harrison.

And they call out 19.

Ohmyfuckinggod. "C'mon, twenty-three. Do twenty-three and I swear, I'll never eat junk food again. C'mon, man. C'mon."

Nicky complains with basso meows, because her hand's stopped doing its job under his chin and she's usually so good at that. Then he jumps straight up into the air with a hiss and lands in a scrambling run, heading for the bedroom closet, because she's thrown the bag of chips at the television and she's jumping and yelling way too loud for it to be a good thing.

So now, here she is a Lotto winner. Her. Sitting in her bedroom, shaking. Her feet gone numb. There's a hollow feeling behind her forehead. *Shit. What now?*

An answer comes: *I have no idea.* Nicky slinks over from the shadows of the closet and crawls up onto the bed, willing to forgive, lobbying for a head scratch. Her fingers rub the backs of his ears and then the length of his long bumpy spine to his elevated rump.

She picks up a pen and her notebook from the nightstand, but moves off the bed to sit on the floor, setting her back against the bedroom wall. Looks at the notebook and giggles.

No.1. Don't tell anyone.

Half an hour later Harrison's lunch cooler hits the counter with a *bang,* and she hears the dragging of the bong across the kitchen table. She has twenty-five numbered lines written in the notebook on her lap.

Harrison doesn't come down the hall and Christina's way too nervous to go into the kitchen. She's sure it's written all over her face. Like the first time with James in her bedroom last summer. Harrison knew just by being in the same house. She can't hide anything from him. *God. What'll I do? God.*

She crawls over to the bed and grabs for the headboard, tosses her pen and notebook on the mattress and huffs her way upright. Tiptoes and pulls the chain to turn on the overhead fan light. Then she studies her face in the mirror. *God. I'm rich.* She giggles. Puts her hand over her mouth-to hold it all in.

Oh shit! It comes to her: no more junk food. Harrison'll know something's up for sure. *But I swore. I heard me. No more junk food if I win. Shit. What was I thinking?*

Nicky pushes the notebook and her pen around on the bed and then takes the pen in his mouth and tries slinking out of the bedroom with it. She lets him. What about the guy who won, and his granddaughter OD'd? She's thinking about Harrison's bong. The occasional speedball he does, when his pal Danny comes by, thinking she doesn't know about it. Or the winners who got sued, or who're on food stamps now. No. She's not gonna tell anyone. Not even Harrison.

Her wins to date have been few and small. $50 was the biggest. She slowly sinks to the floor with her back against the bed now. *I'll look stuff up at work on the computer; see what all I'm in for. I don't even remember how big this pot is, or what taxes'll be. Or how long it takes to get a payout.*

She remains there in a slump until her legs feel like they're falling asleep. Then she tilts until her cheek is on the rag rug. She folds an arm up under her head and uses the other to shield her eyes from the fan light.

Gina knows about two of the numbers, but not the other ones. *Maybe I'll take her to lunch anyway. But no cigs for Matt. Okay, maybe a carton. Maybe. Wow.* She can hear

Harrison switching the light off in the hallway. He calls out a goodnight. Nicky pads back in to snuggle for a while.

At 2 o'clock, she's still lying there; wide-awake, immobile dawn off by a few more hours. The song her mother always used to sing her to sleep each night goes through Christina's head. Billy Joel. Even though now, without knowing it, it's really her own voice that runs in her head. It's been nearly 10 years.

She sits up. Nicky on her other side, sprawled on his back, belly up, front paws curled, legs spread wide. *I could get a camera*, she thinks. She just sits. Doesn't get up to go to bed, instead surveying her room from floor level view. But her eyes are focusing on years ago.

Remembering the one morning when she crawled into her mother's big waterbed to find Harrison there. A new guy. Not nearly as old as some of the others. He smiled at her, raising a finger to his lips, titled his head at her snoring mom, and whispered, "Still sleeping."

She liked his sandy hair. The way he pulled one side of the sheet up over her mother's bared back. Gentle. Held out his hand for a shake. Serious. Courteous. Even at three years old Christina could see this one might be different. She decided to test him. Pushed down hard at the foot of the bed, to make it undulate. And Harrison gripped the headboard and made a funny face, panicked, afraid of being tossed out on the next wave. The sun from the high window warmed her bare feet, the red scar on her ankle still shinny and new. "You like French toast?" he whispered, and Christina was a goner.

Her room swims back into focus and she lets out a long breath. *I won. Wow.*

Wipes her eye. For a moment, she can't stop herself thinking: *What good is it? Mom's still dead. I still live here on Hell Ave. Harrison's still so miserable.*

Harrison and Mom. And Christina is suddenly four years old and back there again. Like a video she'd saved to Favorites on YouTube; she can watch as many times as her heart can press Play.

Sitting on Harrison's lap in the big chair, while he looked through all his Car and Truck, and Off-Roading magazines. A Saturday ritual. Like hot chocolate milk for bad boo-boos and the special blue quilt for stomachaches. The two of them taking turns pointing to the brightest of the color pictures. Harrison turning pages back to look again if she asks.

"Oooo, a Winch," she mimics. "Oooo." His big hands tapping shinny bumpers, and fire-truck-red metal toolboxes, eyes shining. "I'm gonna get one of them." Like walking through a toy store.

Her mother smiling from the kitchen, not trying very hard to lure Christina from his lap. Even when she'd found he'd taught Christina to say "Oh, yeah. Nice ta-tas." Snapping her own thigh with a dishtowel and asking with a laugh, "What're you doing to my kid, Harrison? Trying to make a boy out of her?"

That laugh fades and now Christina bites at her lip. "I gotta face it. I won this." A big win. Now the only thing to do is figure out how to live being happy. She lets out a short breath and scratches her hair until her scalp tingles. "This is all coming off. No matter what."

Christina's wishes are like dreams she can't remember in the morning. Hidden. Just out of reach. Happy is a hard concept for her. She lived with her mother alone, before Harrison. Then with them both. And now with Harrison, alone. Three years of Mama. Seven of a real family, and nearly ten of grief. Christina jokes to herself: The Bad, the Heaven, and the Limbo. Nothing follows a pattern. No telling what might come next, or how long it'll last.

The floor's hard and she shifts her butt to get more comfortable. It doesn't dawn on her to go lie on the bed, where the softness is. This is one of her problems. Letting herself have what she wants, or even needs. She's lived under Harrison's last name so, so long, but her mom never really changed it in court. So she'll show the birth certificate, and get the Lotto payout from the win in her birth name. Nothing like Christina's current one. "No one will figure out it was me."

At two, Christina's biggest wish was to talk right. So that Mama would understand when she pulled on her skirt, trying to get her to see she needs to go to the potty chair. Now.

The swats and the shame were unbearable. If only Christina had the words. If only. But then she did have them. And still there was a reason for a swat. For more shame.

"C'mer, please," Mama said in the calmest of voices and a young Christina, standing the beam of light in the dimness of the kitchen, knew right then how much trouble she'd caused—with Mama, the softer the voice the bigger the punishment. Christina took a step closer. The big clock with the pots of daisies on its face ticked and echoed in the stillness. A standoff; no other noises.

There's no smile or sighing, no shaking of Mama's head in admiration now. No laughing. Dead serious. No slack. "This is a lesson you need to learn, baby. Not a punishment you need to get. Understand?" But Christina didn't understand. Not at all. Not even now.

The amount is unbelievable, even after the taxes. *Nobody should have this kind of dough,* she thinks. It's insane. The scariest thing that comes to her is the life she can have now that this is real. And now, here she has to be brave and deal with the fact that she's won this thing. *Her.* The one who purposely never kept things in her pockets.

Her list is more of things to do than it is things to buy. Christina's not one for big consumption except for eating. She's much happier with self-denial. Her model is Harrison and his cherished Bong; things can end up owning you.

She's seen this and it's turned her 180º from his example. Too much, too many things, smacks of being dependent on stuff. And as her life so far has taught her, self-reliance is the only type of dependence Christina's interested in.

Come Saturday, after the payout, the first thing she does is check her list. Number 1 is a given, but other than keeping the win a secret she hasn't a clue where to start. So she closes her eyes. Circles above the pad with an outstretched finger then plops it down on the page:

No.4 – Pay off the house for Harrison.

This one so contradicts item No.1 in the 'don't tell anybody' category. Hummm. So what she does is sock away $80,000 in a savings account, drawing 5% APY, a term she had to look up and read about. But now she gets it. She found the rate online during her lunchtime at the paper. The mortgage payoff is now as good as done. She won't say anything just yet to Harrison. It'll be his retirement fund.

At the paper it's Beverly on the line. From Distribution's IT department. Accounting always gets a ring on Fridays when someone calls to make sure everyone is off the system for backups to start. Beverly has the nasty habit of believing she's god-like. Never asks nicely when she can command; doesn't care to know if there's an issue on your end. Christina hates it when she's the one to pick up Beverly's call on Fridays.

"Get everyone off and do it now." No *hi there*. No, *this is Beverly calling.*

"Two of us are still doing inputs for end of month, can you give us another—" she looked to Irene and Teresa, who flashed five fingers, three times. "—fifteen more minutes?"

"It's Friday, sweetie. Backup happens no matter what. You don't know that yet?"

It's the 'sweetie' that gets Christina. "But—"

Beverly continues, "Screw any of your buts, babe. Get off the system. Now."

"But—"

Beverly's headed to the top of Olympus, she lets out one long sigh and demands: "Do you know just who it is you're talking to here?"

Christina shoots back, "Do YOU know who you're talking to?"

"No." Beverly answers, "I don't."

"Well, we're working here. Wait the god-damned fifteen minutes or go fuck yourself, Beverly." And Christina hangs up the phone.

The other girls don't know whether to crap, wind their watches, or go blind. Teresa, who never wears pants to work, or goes without stockings or a slip no matter the weather, is chanting, "Oh, shit. Oh, shit. Oh my fucking god. Shit."

Christina reaches into her lower drawer and pulls out her keys and bus pass. Leaves the chip-clip thingy there for the next girl. "I'm sorry ladies." She gives a little good-bye waggle with her fingers. Her eyebrows go up, down. Feels genuinely bad about it. "Gina, we'll go out for lunch as soon as I can."

And she's out the door of Accounting and headed down the hall to HR. For a talk about where to send her last check. Up ahead, down the corridor, she can hear their phone ringing already.

Monday morning, she wants desperately to roll over and go back to sleep, but Christina hears Harrison in the kitchen and knows she has to get up and act like everything's normal. Too bad falling off the face of the earth wasn't on her list.

In front of the fridge, she asks "What d'you feel like for dinner?" Sets a can down for Nicky. Almost forgets the muffin, then makes the save and grabs one from the fridge.

"How 'bout I make sure to get out early and swing by and pick you up? We can go see some movie, sneak in some soda cans. Grab something from Panda Express after."

God.

"I'm thinking about no more eating out. Cutting the junk food out too." Christina stares down at the muffin she's holding and laughs, tossing it into the trash. Whole. She can hear the loose chocolate chips rattling down.

Harrison blinks. "You okay?" his forehead a furrow.

"Sure."

She gets off the bus three stops away from her house, pretty sure Harrison has finally left for work. Jaywalks across the street and makes her way back home.

She's bored out of her mind; she's been working since

work experience class in high school, age fifteen. Today, after the subterfuge, her only thought while unlocking the front door is flopping back into bed now that she's fooled Harrison.

Week after week she picks up the newspaper from the lawn on the way back indoors. One day Christina actually sits at the kitchen table and reads the damn thing. There's no reason for the ad to catch her eye but it does:

> OFFICE WORK: QUIRKY ENVIRONMENT. P/T. GREAT FOR STUDENTS OR CASUAL WORKERS. FLEX HOURS. SOME NON-TRADITIONAL BENEFITS. CALL STELLA.

So Christina sets down her cup of tea and reaches for the phone.

Christina's ready with a list of qualifications and Gina's extension number at the paper, so this Stella won't call HR and get the truth about Beverly's last phone call. But the woman on the line just asks two questions: "Can you dress appropriately for an upscale office?" And, "Do you mind working on your own?"

With a *definitely* and a *definitely not* from Christina, the voice on the line asks what time can she make it in for an interview. And that's it. Christina hangs up and looks at the pad on her lap. 9:00 A.M. Tomorrow. She thinks she knows the address.

"We're what you call a Virtual Office." Stella is explaining. "I started out small. Mass mailings, ads. Fax and phone answering services out of my apartment. But then it dawned on me," Stella spreads her hands to the office behind Christina's chair. "Presentation is everything. So I opened this place."

She goes on explaining about stuff that makes Christina's head spin. Clients who are downsizing from bigger offices, ones who are upgrading from using a post-office box. Christina lets it all wash over her, waits for an opening and a recognizable question she can answer.

"We're providing low-risk alternatives to renting for the small guy just starting out." Stella ticks off on her fingers. "Corporate image on the cheap, proxies for mail and parcel collections."

"As a virtual office, you workers really have nothing to do but look like this is a busy place. Get it?" Christina nods. "You're part of what I'm renting out. I get some shady folks here and there as clients, but I weed 'em out pretty quickly. For the most part it's all on the up and up."

Christina thinks to herself: *Work, almost.* Then she thinks back to the paper, and Beverly. Her bleeding fingers, she figures, *Hell lady, you guys could be a front for organized crime, and I'd take you over The Outrage any day.*

She knows she'll take the job as easily as she knows with the payout she has no need to take it at all. Maybe that's the draw. Stella rises from her chair and pulls her nice jacket from the back of the door, "C'mon. I'll show you around." And Christina follows her into the dazzling office with all the faux-busy workers.

"Here's how it works. You come to work dressed in office attire. Piercings to a minimum. We set you at a desk which will have a PC on it. You're allowed to do anything you want on the PC within reason. Porn is the biggest no-no—that disturbs your neighbors, but we have guidelines you'll get if you take the job."

Stella's back to ticking things off as she walks Christina around the desks and offices. "No speakers if you listen to music. Earphones only and they have to be the bud type." Christina must look like she doesn't understand because Stella stops to elaborate, "less obvious."

"We might, on occasion, have a spot of actual work for you to do. But not often. The four of us permanent staff handle most of that. You'll get the overflow from the phones, mostly. But anytime you walk through the office you must have a prop in your hand. We provide you guys with file folders, clipboards, mugs for each desk."

She waves her hand at a bank of desks where four girls sit. "Anytime you're sitting at a desk you are sitting upright, nothing sloppy, this slouching thing happens a lot for the kids who play that RPG stuff. Also, no laughing way too loud. If there are clients in with their own customers, then no loud chatting with your neighbors—and I get the say of what's too loud."

A girl looks up from a desk they're passing and smiles.

"And she's always listening, too."

Stella nods and continues down another hallway, Christina trailing: "Some of these people are grad students trying to write dissertations. Novelists who can't concentrate at home in their bathrobes. Those types we charge for the PC time. The rest, like you, a half dozen now, we pay. You get the idea, right?" Christina feels like she's taken a sip of water from a fire hose, but she nods. *Right.*

The upshot is, Stella gives her the job. Monday through Wednesday, nine-thirty to four, with a half-hour lunch. Stella shows her the lunchroom on her way out, points to a tri-colored chart, and says, "We have killer potlucks here. Benefits-wise, we pay for Pharmacy prescriptions and you get a Costco card if you want one." Stella pats the filled W-4 form and shakes Christina's hand, "Welcome aboard."

Chapter Three

HER MOTHER'S FACE dims as Christina's eyes flutter open. Nicky is snuggled up close to her side, a furry radiator, and the TV is on; some infomercial. She's on the sofa. It must be 3 or 4 in the morning.

She blinks and sits up. Stretches. Not sure which day it is. Thursday? Friday? As Christina drags herself off the sofa and down the hall to her room, she's not sure she likes the fact she doesn't have to know.

The sun is up and Nicky lays a gentle paw on her cheek, a reminder: *There's no can on the floor, Ma'am. Sorry to be a bother, but, Meow.*

Christina reaches for the list on her headboard. She's been ignoring it for weeks. But there's nothing else to do, so it's calling to her and this time she decides to answer. She struggles to sit upright. Nicky waits at the door, glancing back, hopeful. Again with the closed eyes, again with the finger dropped at random:

No.3 Art Supplies for Harrison.

She's not sure if she can do this one and not confess about the payout. Not sure she wants to do any confessing that might lead to him figuring out about the new job at Stella's. She's not sure she can fess up to what she said to Beverly. His birthday isn't till October. But that's where her finger fell… Art for Harrison.

Oh, shit. What the hell.

She already hates herself for giving up all the chips and sodas and candy. There's even more hate for wimping out and not cutting her hair like she thought she would. What's one more thing? She'll figure out a lie to tell about the art supplies somehow.

Twenty-five minutes and a hot shower later, Christina watches the bus that's heading for downtown pass her by. She's taken to walking everywhere now.

Too much art stuff to choose from, and no idea where to start. Harrison talked a lot about an easel with a drawer. Something to take out into the desert on weekends, to catch the sunrise and sunsets. But he talks about a lot of stuff. Stuff that rarely gets touched anymore, once he starts it then leaves off for some good reason. Ten years of unfinished business.

Like the white VW camper in the back yard. Up on blocks since she turned eighteen; since the week she took off and was gone for a time. Harrison's rusted old baby for how long? Then poof—just because she'd gone for a walkabout, he lost heart about restoring it. A shift in mood that somehow became tied to her going. A little death to string up his heart like the larger death seven years before that. Like she'd become the one to hang the blame on now. Like Harrison's whole life after her mother died now ended up Christina's responsibility. Who wouldn't have taken off?

Christina spends time questioning the store manager, and then decides on two items; a kit for using charcoal to create portraits and a deluxe tripolar French easel; a wooden one that combines a sketch box, easel, and canvas carrier in one. Art for days with this puppy. It's Van Gogh or no go if Harrison can't get some joy out of this.

"Holy Shit! This's a Huntington!" Harrison can't stay seated in his recliner once he opens his eyes and sees the easel, now with a bright blue bow on it. The rest of the evening isn't much more articulate than that. "HO-LEE CRAP!" that's about it.

The Draw Today Kit floors him even more. He opens it up and spreads the charcoal and grids out on the floor to see all its bits all at once. Christmas come early. "A video too— Cool!" Christina couldn't be happier in his tongue-tied joy. "Fuckin' shit. Thanks, man. Thanks."

Christina, with her legs up on the couch, wishes she had a Big Gulp. Watches Harrison down on the floor, and smiles. "Art for days, huh?" He doesn't even think to ask about how she got it for him.

It's Danny at the door, Harrison's connection. Usually he calls first, so Harrison can make sure Christina's gone if they're going to be doing harder stuff than just smoking. Most folks call him Bud, for obvious reasons. But he's really Danny… The Duke of Meth, Dope, Speedballs, anything pharmaceutical. Imperial Valley; SW region. Harrison steps to the side and Danny slides into the house, waves to Christina who's moved to the kitchen. He lopes over to the sofa, plops himself down.

Harrison's on the way to pull them a couple of beers from the fridge. Taps her shoulder as he goes, "What we got for snacks?"

"I'll get something going." And he's back to the living room. She can hear the recliner's swoosh of exhaled air as Harrison lands in it.

Christina moves to the other cabinet. Stealth. Strains to hear. Nothing. And by what they're not saying, Christina knows what's coming. She pulls a cast iron Comal from a lower shelf and knocks it on the stove burner setting it down, the clang echoing. She starts frying up some quesadillas.

Danny only bothers to sit on the sofa if he wants to get Harrison to come do speedballs with him back at Danny's trailer. Otherwise Danny always sits at the kitchen table, drags a bag of dope from his pocket and they fire up the bong. Standard procedure. Danny thinks of himself as a 'Behind the Scale' kinda guy; won't do his own product most of the time. A bong hit, sure, that's just a salesman courtesy.

Keep calm, she tells herself. *Maybe this time he won't go.*

Harrison's showing off the easel and the portrait kit. He's picked up Christina's phrase, been repeating all weekend long now. "Art for days, buddy-boy. Art for fuckin' days here." So happy. *Maybe,* she thinks, *maybe it'll be okay.*

A stack of old, old songs, from before even Harrison or Danny were born, blasts on the stereo. Harrison is big on aged vinyl. Has stuff from as far back as 1960. Nothing scratched or warped though, cherry stuff. But ancient. The lyrics all so corny.

The guys sit and smoke. Knock back the bottles of chilled beers that Christina sets in front of them. Down the hefty quesadillas she's fried. The song that's playing makes her feel a bit poetic, as she stands with a hand on the back of the sofa, considering getting out of there. She watches the emptying platter on the coffee table, thinking, *like wolves at a dump.*

The bullshitting's at normal levels: High. Like any old guys do on Sunday afternoons; while they ignore the TV and some dead singer croons a bunch of ballads. Love songs running under the tough talk every time these two get together.

But her laughing dies when she hears from the sofa, "I'm outta here, dude." Heavy feet to the door, a 'Thanks for the grub, youngster!' shouted at the kitchen. Then, lower, the offer: "Plenty. You wanna come on over."

Silence, both in the kitchen and out at the front door. Christina, frozen at the table, can all but feel Harrison glancing over his shoulder, checking his tone, some mumbled variation of: nah. But virtually telegraphing: 'Okay if I go play with the guys?'

Then it's, "Yeah. Yeah, why not? Just wait a sec, bro." And the music stops dead.

For her entire six-hour shift, three or four days a week, the girl in the pod next to her at Stella's (a woman, really, she's easily into her fifties), Jean, traverses all the soap sites online. And it's not just the shows that she's recording while she's here. Jean swims in all her soap trivia and show history like it's her amniotic sac.

They'd got to talking once. And it was quite poetic how Jean put it, how the soaps were the world that didn't hurt, for all the rapes and angst, and broken marriages. "It helps me to forget," was how she put it, and Christina didn't want to pry about what. She was missing Gina, back at the Outrage. And Jean seems genuinely glad to see her every day Christina comes in to sit next to her pod. They laugh at the same jokes, most of the time.

Once, Christina notices Jean actually hugging herself as she enumerates the years she's been hooked, "I watched Ryan's Hope in real time. July seventh nineteen seventy-five, January thirteenth, nineteen eighty-nine. I was seven when it came on." Her eyes glow, as though a saintly visitation from Fatima's displayed on her terminal. Christina nods, mouths 'Wow'.

"Tina." A low whisper, "Hey! … Tina!" Jean's face is a basket of joy. "Pick up a clipboard and come see this " That self-hug thing again. She refuses to call Christina by anything but Tina, and the rest of the pod mates at the other three desks follow suit. She's been rechristened.

"'Kay. Gimme a sec." Christina minimizes all her open screens and reaches for her prop. They all need to be especially on the ball today as there's a Client group up at Rose's desk, with customers in tow. A glance takes in a taller woman in a teal suit leaning in and asking something. Rose smiles and checks her log book. Stands and comes around her desk to point the three of them to Conference Room B, the one that has the glass wall with a wide swipe of frosted glass about four and a half feet from floor level, so those walking by won't make eye-contact with the clients. Stella's thought of everything.

Rose picks up the P.A. mic at her elbow, announcing, "The one o'clock meeting with OptraMedia is now commencing in Conference Room B." Code for: Sit up and look busy people!

Jean's pointing to her monitor where there's a black and white photo of a girl who looked to be in her early twenties, if that.

"Mary Ryan." Jean breathes with pride.

This Mary Ryan has a strong jaw and stares right into the camera. She's stood at the edge of a cliff, with a blanket-sized shawl wrapped around her shoulders. The photo calls to Christina's mind some dispossessed Celtic queen. The sea below her to the left crashes onto a rocky coastline and a winding craggy road falls away to the right. Beautiful.

Christina sets her pad down and pulls a chair closer to Jean's desk, "Don't know her," she confesses, leaning in. There's something about *this* photo. Jean's shown her other old-time soap folks; women in sequined gowns mostly, or men with teeth too white to be believable. Christina always felt—So what?

But this one. There's something about her. The black and white—is that it? The hint of regal bearing without a sequin in sight? A faint suggestion of a widow's peak at the hairline, the ghost of freckles? No. It's simply the overall handsomeness of the girl, even in black and white. "What show's she in?"

Jean rears back and lands a slug on Christina's arm. Painful. "Don't you tease me!" she hisses, lowers her shoulders, checks behind her to make sure Stella isn't near. "Ryan's Hope! Jeezie-Weezie, Tina, do you, like, live under a rock or what?"

Then Jean clicks her mouse and drops down her Favorites List. She heads straight to some site and there it is: Ryan's Hope. The site has everything: History, Cast, Summaries, Characters, Photos and more. Jean clicks link to link, chatting the whole time. But there's not enough of the girl.

The photos are mostly of the rest of the cast. Out of the corner of Christina's eye, Denise is giving a sign, Stella sighting: 9 o'clock. Christina stands and grabs her pad.

"Email me that link."

Jean's been more than conscientious—aside from the show's fan site, she forwarded a slew of Ryan's Hope videos from YouTube. Christina has to laugh. Jean's introduction with that first photo was for the soap character's name—not the actress: Kate Mulgrew.

Christina surfs the Ryan's Hope site, pulled by something in that girl's face. A missing portion of her life seems to have clicked into place with a single photo of a girl on a cliff, the wind blowing her hair behind her.

She continues to scan the site, ignoring all the words, only watching for pictures, skipping the guys named Malcolm and Andrew. She feels a shift just under her breastbone—like her lungs have been ancient bellows and someone so strong, so able, has unexpectedly, finally, spread those bellows wide and for once she can breathe.

She says to herself, before dropping off to sleep each night, "If I can keep it a secret, it can't get out of hand." Christina dreams of shifting circumstances and sudden poverty; sometimes she wakes up smiling every once in a while. Like this morning.

A new day. Nicky's been fed. Christina closes her eyes, takes a breath and circles with her finger above the notebook, then points and drops her hand.

No.7 Learn Stuff. That's a good one.

She finds the listing. Imperial Valley College. Christina thought there would be others in the area. But she doesn't click on the link.

She won't delve into this stuff at Stella's; that would make things more real somehow.

Christina writes down the address she finds and then searches the bus route maps for the best way to get there in an afternoon, to look around. Just in case old IVC has something to spend some dough on.

On the bus she dozes and dreams of finding at least five colleges. In her dream, Christina visits them all. In their campus libraries, all the catalogs are up in a floor above, no matter where she goes. She tries scribbling down all the subjects she's longed to learn about but, in the dream, she can't name any of them.

Then she's walking into the dream bookstores like she has the right to be there, but she's immediately pointed to another flight of stairs to climb.

In the end she has a stack of textbooks so tall she decides to buy a handcart too, like she's watched students dragging around. She's grinning like all mad crazy as she boards the last bus—heading for home. She flashes her bus card. And sinks into a seat. Heaven.

A bump in the road wakes her and she opens her eyes, back here in 'real time', as Jean calls it. But refreshed. Satiated. She's gone maybe 12 blocks but she feels like she's gone miles. What a great vision. Has to be a good sign, she figures. *Has to be.* Christina rings the bell when her stop comes up.

There in the school's library, Christina surfs the IVC site, reads about The Facilities: The Ray White Tool Distribution Center, Automotive technology. The Infant Care Center, their Lab-type department to train for Early Child Education. Their print shop. She keeps looking but only picks out the words like Industrial Tech, Agriculture, Electronics, Auto Body, Welding. Cool skills to learn, but where are the classes that teach the knowledge?

She decides to skip going on a campus walkabout. She's suddenly sleepy. Christina wishes she had that dream back, never once considering that she could have enrolled at any one of those schools in her dream. Misses that entirely.

At home she looks at her list again, but doesn't cross No.7 off yet.

No.6 – Buy one NICE thing for myself.

It doesn't go against her nature to dream but acting on those dreams is something that pains her. Cuts deep and leaves her heart on a tilt. Her breath suddenly struggles through a smaller, constricted airway. She just can't bring herself to press 'Add to cart'. She wipes her hands on her nicer linen skirt and leans away from the monitor. The rest of her list remains untouched. Her feet, in her office pumps, feel like they've fallen asleep.

It's like the doing, the owning, would burn her fingers. She puts No.6 on hold just a little bit longer.

At least there's the other websites. The ones without shopping carts and view basket links. There's that Kate Mulgrew site from Ryan's Hope. All those wonderful pictures from the soap opera. She skims past all the words and goes only for finding black and white photos. Collecting them is nice, so maybe that's a way to have No.6.

Christina makes sure every workday she's dressed her best, and then sits back and plays. This is definitely her year. But then the guilt rises. She calls Gina at the Outrage: "Hey girl, sorry I didn't call sooner. Wanna do a lunch sometime next week?"

A squeal in reply, "I thought I'd lost you for good!" And they plan on a Mexican place.

Christina's not all that good on the phone with girls; the talk devolves too quickly for her taste. So she promises, "Thursday after next. Noon." Acts like someone here in the office is calling her: "Gina. Gotta go. See ya. Friday, yep, I know, not this one, the next. Yep. Uh-huh. 'Kay gotta go now. Um-Bye."

Denise, another pod-mate asks her what she's interested in. "On the Web," she adds.

"Books." Christina decides. Nods her head yes, like she's just made her mind up about it. "Learning stuff."

Jean, the north point of the pod is listening to the discussion, not buying it, thinks Christina's too young for books. "Books are for fuddies. There must be something else." Teases her by telling Denise, "Really, Tina spends all her time here checking out Hotmail dotcom."

"Why would I need an email account?" Christina asks, "We get one here for free?"

And the girls giggle. Jean pointing down to her own lap: "H-O-T-M-A-L-E-D-O-T-C-O-M. Silly."

Denise adds, "Primarily, 'cause it gives ya the tingles."

Christina just shakes her head: Girls.

She opens up Amazon and reconsiders treating herself to No.6 and buying something she's had her eye on, something called the Science Masters Series. A fifteen-book set. She likes the blurb that promises a range of disciplines, from astrophysics to zoology. Talk about tingles.

"Chrissie. Wake up. C'mon—you got a call from work. Up baby." It's not a dream. Harrison is in her room, shaking her awake. He never calls her Chrissie. Except when things are sad. Oh Shit. Stella's office. Oh, *shit*.

Rose is on the line. Can Christina make it in today? Knows it's a Saturday, "We have this ginormous CD mailer thing to get out. Please?" Could really use the help. Double time. "Stella says she'll buy the bagels and OJ if that helps at all."

Christina sets the phone back down and Harrison waves away anything she wants to say, "We can do this after you get back. Go on. Get ready. I can drive you."

Chapter Four

L IKE IT ALWAYS was with her mother, the punishment from Harrison is a serving of disappointment. Silence. On the drive down to the office the corners aren't taken too sharply. The stops at the lights don't jar, and once the light's green again the take offs aren't abrupt. Even the windshield wipers are set on low against the drizzle.

And the gentleness of it all pounds home the poise and character Harrison and her mom expected from her. The two things she's always managed to fail at delivering.

She swipes at her hair, and it dawns on her she kept it long because that's how her mother wore it. How Harrison likes girl's hair to be. Long, loose. Tradition. Like driving so cautiously when he's pissed-off or it's rainy like today is.

Her mind goes to spite from all the passivity in the truck: *The day you kick it, buddy, this is all coming off. And I'm learning to drive, too. Bet on it.*

Her head pounds the whole time her hands are moving at work, stuffing CDs into sleeves, followed by the flyers into the flat packages, the packages into boxes, and boxes into cartons; her mind is free to wander.

And it clicks onto replay again: standing in that beam of light in the dim kitchen, knowing she'd been bad, but not quite how Mama is judging the bad. Lots of trouble, she knew that much. Big Trouble. Mama has her standing there. No sitting, no discussing. The big clock ticks and ticks and ticks. And still Christina stood. Trying to figure out what it is that went wrong. A stand-off. Mama wants the same answers.

Finally. "Baby. That's my ring. Harrison gave that to me when we got married last month. Understand. It's our wedding ring. From him to me." She let out a breath and stroked Christina's long, long hair. "My ring, Chrissie, not yours."

Christina, at seven, can't figure out how come Harrison only wants Mama to have the ring. Why not give a ring to her? That's why she took it and hid it in the pocket of her jeans to begin with. Mama's explaining that this is all about the ring. When it isn't the ring Mama really wanted. Mama wanted Harrison. And Christina always thought of Harrison as hers. She's the one who found him while Mama slept.

Harrison waits out front of the office. Just slightly buzzed. Drives again with the utmost of care on the slick streets. The oncoming lights on the wet April pavement skew the divider lines and he taps his breaks more than he really needs to. Nervous. Avoiding all the ghosts the rain's brought on. Pulls into their driveway and sets the parking brake, removes the key from the ignition then just sits.

She knows right then she'll be going. It's just a matter of time. Knows it like she knows their breath will soon fog the windshield. She sees Nicky's nose peeking from behind the blinds, then his fat furry paw in the picture window. White. For some reason she thinks, *I'll have to vacuum the drapes.*

"Got some questions, slugger. You up for that?"

Seven. All over again. Christina's twisting her foot, just like then, "Okay."

"You're not working at the paper anymore?"

"No."

"Any reason to talk about that?"

"None."

She looks out the window; the sun, now low enough to skirt under the rain clouds, cuts a swatch of fading light on the driveway next to them, between the two houses. Doesn't touch the truck. Dimness here.

Dimness like the kitchen that day, when it all came clear to her. From that day on Christina, bowed under the hurt Mama felt, soaked up all that pain of disappointments. And the dimness, and the too-loud ticking of the kitchen clock. She's like a dry sponge, ready to take it all in till she's saturated. Walked around emotionally waterlogged and physically heavy from that moment on.

At seven years old she made two promises to herself: Nothing in her pockets—never again. And to never want someone for herself, either. It's a cheat. Like wishing for a pony before blowing out all the birthday candles. There's never a pony. Ever.

Harrison's doing that sighing thing. Soft and quiet. She can hear the rain on the truck's roof. "You're working this new place, but not all the time. Not all like you been acting."

"Right," she swallows. One syllable. So hard to enunciate.

"And what's this?" He's pulled her statement from the bank out of his jeans pocket, the envelope slit open but the contents still folded inside.

She opens her mouth but nothing comes out. Tries again and shivers, crosses her arms to grab her shoulders, huddles. No warmth. Asks a question of her own, "Harrison, can we go inside first? I'm freezing my tits off out here."

"How much?"

Christina doesn't think to hide her grin. She tells him.

Harrison sits back and reaches for his bong. "Hy-a-mucka."

"Yep." She stands up from the kitchen table and moves to get the passbook he's missed finding, up behind a basket on top of the fridge. Shows Harrison the mortgage dough. "It's all paid off. If you want it." Sits down again and slips a cuticle into her mouth.

Harrison swats at her hand. "Quit that." He whistles, low, "Man. What you gonna do?"

"About what?"

"*Do.* Baby, what are you gonna do now?"

"Well," She ignores thinking about No.7 and No.6. "I paid into this account. And I bought you the art stuff…" It sounds lame said out loud like this.

Being at work with access to the net all day leads Christina to reconsider Harrison's advice that what's needed is some seriously conspicuous consumption. In spite of the fact that only eight of the original twenty-five things on her list are things to buy, versus seventeen things to do, she takes the plunge one day and buys a Mac laptop. Fully loaded. Her eighteen hours a week online at Stella's fall far too short now that Harrison knows. Now that there are the black and white Ryan's Hope pictures. Now that she can breathe right.

Now Christina can do a few more things for him. So she buys him a laptop, too. Loads it with software for graphics and music editing. Tells the guy she buys it from, Brian, from the paper, "Can you set it up so when he turns it on for the first time a great big message crawls across the screen for him to read—from me?"

Brian, says, "Sure. I can do just about anything you want short of a hostile takeover of your local Post Office." He taps some keys and she's looking at the sudden black screen with no pictures at all, just rows of orange text. He starts right in; seems to know what he's doing from the get-go. Shoulders aren't tense at all. Freaky. He shoves the keyboard over to her and says, "Key in what you want him to see."

So Christina pauses a second then begins typing. Brian even lets her choose the font when she's done.

"That stuff you did. With the black screen. Can anyone learn that?"

"Command line stuff? Sure. You can buy books on that. Take courses. It's candy."

"Can you show me?"

"What's it worth to you?" he jokes.

She thinks back to what she guesses he's earning at the paper, "How about your hourly rate the Beast pays?"

"Whudja' do, Christina? Win the lottery that day you blew?"

"Oh, yeah. Right, Brian. Fantasize much?"

She's thinking about the websites she surfs. About how after Brian shows her the black screen maybe he can help her with building her own website; with only photos in black and white. Like Harrison's record collection; just all the first-rate, vintage stuff.

Why fight it? She asks herself at least three times daily. Christina's hooked. Though, underneath, just a tad worried about it. It's not like she wants to be like Jean. Obsessed. It's just that she's found such a fresh face with this Kate Mulgrew person; so confident, lively looking, and—pretty.

All that reverie is slowed when Stella calls her away from

the pods to her office.

"Got a minute?"

Christina looks at Jean over the partition and asks Stella, "Sure. Need me to bring something for notes?" That gets a *sure* right back, then she's up following Stella down the hallway and past conference room B. The pod is struck quiet and wondering. Not many get fired. Stella isn't like that; so what could possibly be up?

"Think we fooled them?" Stella leans back in her La-Z-Boy office chair, hoisting her feet up on the desk. She's been let in on Christina's secret and they spend time looking into finance 101 matters on the web. A crash course that Stella feels every new Lotto winner should have. Not Christina's idea at all. Like having a big sister shop for camping gear with you for the Graduation trip you've planned all during high school.

It was easy to say yes to the help; Stella's generosity was too genuine not to accept.

"Dude."

"Hey Danny. Howzit?"

"Good. Good."

"C'mon in."

Fuck. Christina raises her voice from the kitchen, "Harrison! I'll be back later!" Grabs her bus pass and slips out the back door. Walks around the house to the street. *I'm out of there. If they're doing speedballs, not even bothering to go to Danny's...* and that's the only reason Danny ever makes it over to Heil Avenue, unscheduled.

The bus takes its time coming and besides, Christina has no idea where to go anyway.

She remembers her mom, way before Harrison. Being chatted up on a bus. It's maybe one of Christina's first memories. A great big tall black guy. Willis. Them acting like they knew each other all along. Her mother showing Christina off in her little bunny suit. "Say hi there to the nice man, Chrissie." And the big man, smiling, saying, "You can see whose eyes she got, Viv."

Willis—that guy on the bus. Now he owns the BBQ place, *Word of Mouth*. Best stuff this side of Imperial. Pulled pork and chicken wings to die for. Links and ribs and sweet potato pie. You can smell the BBQ four blocks away on windy days if you come up from the west. And the aroma leads you like a dog on a leash to his front door. There's always been something about Willis that Christina's drawn to.

When the bus wheezes up to the curb, that's where she heads. Willis is always good for a talk. For a cool down. He's an older guy; has a few years on Harrison. For a while back when Christina was a baby, too young to remember, her mom said she went out with him.

Tall, gotta be nearly six foot. It might be that that draws her. The height. Or maybe Christina just has a thing for older guys who cook. Who knows? Aside from the food there's Willis himself; bald, muscles like a football player, the biggest smile. She just likes hanging out at his place and talking.

She's been coming in here on her own since the 9th

grade. He's like family. One of the folks who acted as pallbearer at the funeral.

The corrugated tin on the walls, the homemade cobbler, "All of it," Willis brags, "homemade 'cept for the burger buns—even the spice mixture I use on the spicy fries, mix it up my own self."

She sits and doesn't talk about what's on her mind. He sits and tells her about making cobbler, like she's never heard this before. Dried fruits vs. canned, popular wisdom versus old-time ways of doing it up right. The precise cinnamon to nutmeg ratio and the secret third spice. Christina keeps that to herself. She will even if Willis forgets to warn her to keep it secret (he never does). She tries real hard not to mention Harrison and what's probably happening right now at home.

Finally, when she's cooled down enough, Willis talks her into a plate of food. "No fries, though, no cornbread," she says.

Willis growls, but rearranges the plate to suit the request. Points a pair of tongs at her and says, "My gran had a saying you know. When it came to girls getting too thin. Man likes some meat on a woman. Leave them bones for the dogs."

Christina doesn't care. Pours iced tea into her mason jar, instead of soda. Leaves off adding sugar.

At home Harrison takes one look at the storm still riding in Christina's eyes and has no trouble at all fessing up: because this time he's turned Danny down.

"So you can drop the scowl. I'm clean, officer. Really."

Christina runs her hands through her tangle of curls and whispers, "Yeah. This time." She thinks the long talk with Willis has calmed her down, but no. She's ready to cry all over again. Swearing that she won't, not anymore; she's not had one bit of junk food of any kind since the win. Things are shifting in her life. Maybe she can't get herself to spend any of the money, but this is going to be one of the things that changes.

Harrison's hands are nervous on the table. Drumming some beat he's got running though his system. "I didn't do it for a reason. I mean—I said no because of you."

She looks up. "What a line."

"No really, baby. I see you with all the dough and you're not doing a damn—not doing anything with it. And I think: Is it me? Does she get this need for inertia from me?"

Christina stands and walks away. Leaves the fool to his stories and heads for the living room. Pulling her legs up onto the sofa she tries making herself smaller. Spending. He snuck that in. This is supposed to be about the speedballs with Danny.

But Harrison follows and keeps on going, "Well, baby, see…" But Christina doesn't see. Doesn't see how seeing makes her any different of a person. Harrison gets into the moods to talk about using some of the money and being a better person and Christina can only think about setting her mind in neutral and waiting him out. Her tongue, busy, touches each of her teeth, top and bottom.

The tremendous need to find a mirror, open wide, and count those puppies; *can there really be only 24? That can't be right.* Didn't she read somewhere there were more? Harrison sees her mind is elsewhere. Recognizes that set of shoulder, the slump of spine. She's got none of his genes, but still he sees.

She stares through the living room at the kitchen table, hardly moving her eyes at all. He stops. Because her ears aren't set to receive mode. Like he hasn't ever seen that before. Like this isn't his lot in life all over again.

"Say one more word and I'll just go again." Echoes of Viv; Christina doesn't even know she's doing it to him.

Harrison sighs, flips on the TV and sits back in his recliner. Biding his time. But he knows; *Well not this time. Two wrongs don't have to make a third.*

At work she's made friends and influenced Stella. The girls all point out how she's getting thinner. Denise mentions hand weights, when Christina asks, "What would you do to speed things up some?" The regular staff joins in and ask for Christina's help every once in a while. Her A/R skills. And she's always there when they call.

Jean smiles when Christina comes back from some project, whispering, "Know the difference between an ass-kisser and a brown-noser, Skinny-girl?"

"Nah, Jean. Tell me." Game. Ready for a ribbing. "What?"

"Depth perception." Jean snorts, tapping twice on her desk.

Denise, from the other side of the four desks, chuckles

too; "Excessively funny, Jean. You're a card." Denise has a pop-up box—on her PC's desktop—each morning she's in; Word of the Day. Today's word must be *excessive*; she's used it twice already, and it's not even lunchtime.

Christina just opens her browser and smiles. "Yeah, well. Thank god I wear contacts, girls." And that cracks them up even more. She Googles hand weights and what type of exercises you can do with them. Plans a little purchase. Maybe.

Jean's birthday's coming up; there's a company email from Stella. Subject: DON'T show this to JEAN!!!

Chapter Five

"THAT'S A GOOD point," Christina doesn't mind all the ideas Harrison points out. Lately, she just lets them roll right over her, though she knows this last one *is* a very good point. She likes mentioning how, since he's never up for work anymore, his hair's looking mighty freaky. But she knows it's a point that'll be missed over and over. At least he's willing to keep the money a secret.

Harrison continues, "You could get a bike. That'll be like seven, seven and a half miles in each direction. Put panniers on it. For your office clothes. You're doing great now, but with a bike in the mix you'd get in great shape quick. Great. I mean—if you wanted to. You said no more junk food. Right? You gotta be, what? Down by twelve pounds or so just from that? This seems like the next step for that route, right?"

"I'll check it out." She promises. So he leaves it at that. But his noticing ticks her off. *Dammit.* So she adds, "You doing any painting yet?" Just because she can. Because she knows him. It's a glancing blow, no points at all. Harrison smiles, sad.

"I'm thinking on it. Looking at old snaps from the big hatbox. Maybe one of the two of you. Do it in charcoal after I practice with graphite, first. Yeah. Practice, then do it up right, something twenty-by-twenty-four." His hands spread wide, his chest expanded. "Suitable for framing. You know?"

God. That look. All that fucking hope in his eyes. Makes her feel like shit. The clench in her stomach burns. Christina offers, "Let me go get my laptop. We can see what's out there, bike-wise. 'Kay?"

And he drums his fingers again, making the bong jump. He yells at her back, "Trek. That's a great brand. The Multi-Track. A Hybrid. Finest kind for day to day riding."

But he's out of the loop by several years; the site they find doesn't have multi-track hybrids for women anymore. Harrison laughs, "Well crap." Points to something called the Equinox 7, for Triathlons, "look at this one."

Christina rolls her cursor over the Equinox, the description pops up, at the four-figure dollar amount to the left of the decimal point—she keeps rolling. *It's a bike for Christssake. Not a used car.* "Maybe I'll just stick with upping the number of sit-ups I do at night, add walking around the block three times after dinner. Instead of just the one."

She leaves it at that. And Harrison lets her, though he makes her bookmark the URL. "Never know." But she shakes her head. Knowing. There's got to be better ways to spend a small fortune, than buying a two-thousand-dollar toy.

During a work break in the lunchroom she broaches the subject about a bike with Denise and Daniel.

"I love biking. In Vancouver I used to do it all the time." Daniel slaps at his midsection and the girls try to ignore the jiggle. He's from Phoenix, blonde. A grad student just shy of twenty-five, with an online degree from a University up in Canada.

The program demands he go up twice a year, but he can live anywhere he wants. "Cost of living here in El Centro is cake compared to Seattle or Portland or, the gods forbid, the Bay area. And I really can't be trusted in San Diego with all the sailors. Might get, you know, shanghaied."

Daniel fascinates Denise. But Daniel only has eyes for the novelist he sits next to. Marc. "Bikes." Christina repeats again, trying to keep on topic, "Good idea or bad?"

Marc stands to go refill his coffee mug, "You want to do something like a marathon? Or just get to work?"

"Work."

Denise says, "She wants it for cardio. We figured Daniel'd know about that." She nearly gushes.

"Oh. Well then you don't need a really expensive one. Go online. Do some research?" Daniel's eyes wander over, waiting on Marc.

Denise sees the glance and wilts a bit, playing with her hair. She gives it a second try, "Maybe you can ask your dad, Tina." She can't figure a way to slip in today's word, so they head back to their pod once break's over.

But Christina goes to Willis instead. He'll give good advice. He was the one who'd let her stay for those three days before she decided to leave town for good, back then, at eighteen. Tried talking her into at least calling Harrison, for her own good. But Christina was too dammed stubborn and so Willis just stepped back, fed her and let her sleep on the sofa in his back room.

His wife, Tonette, hadn't said anything while Christina was in the cafe, instead waiting till late at night, but still, her voice echoed down the hall and into the spare room: "Who is this girl? And do you have to be so dammed nice all the time to all these strays?"

"Aw, Tonette," Christina heard, "now baby…"

"Aww Tonette, now baby, shit." And a pot clanged against the range or maybe upside the zinc sink there in the kitchen. The *boonnngggg* cutting into the night, "Damn Willis. What about her daddy?"

Once Christina was out of town, she did phone Willis, for a voice she knew. A way to bolster her going. Tonette picked up. 10:13 p.m., too late for calling someone else's hubby. Christina cut the connection. What else could she do?

Potluck plans; requests that all employees stay later than Jean today, for a quick meeting. Stella had made up a tri-colored chart. Code-named, April Showers. This party was also

Jean's third-year work anniversary too, plus she was one of the older people there. So they were doing it up big. A Funeral motif. Come in your finest mourning.

Everyone had to come in black next Tuesday. "Anyone who doesn't have a black suit or dress can wear a black arm band." Stella's thought of everything. Jean's cake will be baked in the shape of a coffin. "Black and silver balloons?" Someone suggests a visitation guest book too, "Ooo! Yeah."

Conference Room B is full, even though it's past 4 p.m., everyone loves planning this stuff, it seemed. Stella's busy scribbling notes. "Hey, how about a big salad platter like a wreath, y'know, roses made from tomatoes and radish flowers? With a banner on it." Murmurs, *humm…* "How about 'Good Bye To All That'?" Presentation is everything. Christina's suggestion: "It's All Reruns From Now On." Everyone likes that one.

The next day at her desk Christina surfs eBay, finding a cherry condition 10th Anniversary Issue of something called 'Soap Opera Digest' She can't tell for sure that it's a good one, but it was printed in 1985. If nothing else, it's old. Jean should like that.

She emails the link to Denise for reassurance. Watches her eyebrows raise as she reads Christina's message and clicks on the big find. Studies it like they're considering something in a catalog from Sotheby's. When Denise gives a thumbs up, Christina figures she'll just buy the thing outright. Because she has no idea how bidding works. Doesn't have a

PayPal account. And later that day she mails off a money order she gets from the store on the way home.

The notebook list waits and nothing Christina does in her mind makes her spend some of her winnings. But Harrison's suggestions just piss her off. "Later." She can't think now. "It's not like the money's going anywhere."

Harrison gets sly. Opens his laptop and asks, 'What about this?' and says, 'Whoo. Boy, who'd have thought.' and 'Well crap, come see this'. Awe in his voice every time, so she's drawn to go see. But it's always something to buy. Like the Equinox, or worse, a little Vespa. Or a god damned pot from some super fancy place selling kitchen stuff. He points and pronounces the thing like he's introducing her to royalty, "The Le Creuset. Oval Dutch Oven" Emphasis on the Oval.

"Yeah." She replies. Not asking how much. Not looking at all. Well, not lingering when she does look.

"Two and three-fourths Quart size." Harrison adds, enunciating the three-fourths.

"They got anything in the way of knives?" But he doesn't get the hint.

Harrison should've been awake but no one's answering that banging on the front door, so Christina rolls over on the sofa and sits up "Coming!"

A UPS guy. With a foot Christina holds Nicky back from scooting out the door, runs her hand through her hair. "Harrison Paul?" the guy in brown asks. She nods and gently skootches Nicky backwards so she can slip outside Nicky *bar-ooo*'s, denied again. She signs for a huge box.

Slipping back inside she scoops up the cat. The guy walks the box into the house, like he's drawn some slow fat girl for a dance partner, and doesn't mind leading one bit. Leans it up against the hallway wall. It's the size of a small dining room tabletop but about a foot thick. Where's Harrison?

She smiles at the guy, latches the screen door once he's headed back to his truck. She wants desperately to sink back down on the sofa. Wishes she hadn't given up those Cool Ranch chips. But what can you do? A deal's a deal.

Ignores that irritating box. Tries to, at least.

Nothing helps, so she goes and gets one of the new muffins from the fridge; homemade. Heavy as tire irons molded into six-ounce lumps. Flaxseed meal, oat bran, and whole-wheat flour. Walnuts, and shredded carrots and apples. No trans fats. Very irritating. But, well… She washes it down with a teeny can of V-8 juice. And then one of pineapple. A measly 6 ounces, but it counts for another vegetable and one more fruit.

She's about to lie back down on the sofa when it hits her: *Fuck me*, she thinks, *it's a damned bike.*

He must have called up to Borrego Springs and asked for them to ship this. They'd looked and found nothing closer in a full fifty-mile range when they checked for local dealers while they surfed the site that one time. It'd better not be the two-thousand-dollar model. Harrison's not that crazy.

Like naming a ship, it's Harrison's idea that they christen the bike; and Christina doesn't even stop to ponder. She chooses *Kate M.*

When the clerk guy at the bike shop rolls the wine-colored bike out to her, assembled now with the bright golden script on the Trek's down tube and on the top of the fork. The clerk guy asks, "Name it after yourself?"

Christina looks away, down at the riding gloves in the glass case, then up at the hanging jerseys on the wall with all the logos. "No, no." And leaves it at that.

But the decal guy grins, turns and asks Harrison "Voyager? Since it's a Trek and all." Christina has no idea what he means. And Harrison, pulling some bills from his pocket, just tells her, "My treat." He looks at the guy and asks: "What?"

Decal guy studies the two of them with an oblique squint, the type of thing Matt at the 7-Eleven used to do with Christina when she'd buy her ticket each week. Christina feels the judgement in her bones. Probably just sees a stoner and some young chunky chick who'd let the bike go to dust and two flats in a month or three, easy. "You know, Star Trek Voyager. Captain Kathryn Janeway." He points at the bike, and writes with his finger in the air, "Kate M."

Christina feels the hair on her arms rise. Something

dawns on her and she nearly laughs out loud right there in the shop. Shrugs instead and shakes her head. Takes the handlebars like nothing at all is crawling up her spine and resting at the crown of her head. Nothing shining. Nothing wonderful.

Carefully she wheels the beautiful bike past all the displays, heading to the door and towards the truck. For the first time ever she recognizes a swing in her hip as she walks.

Oh Wow.

Hears the register ring and the clerk calling out to Harrison, "She'll like just pedaling around, nothing strenuous. Make sure she keeps it in an easy gear and she'll be fine."

So that moment leads her to color photos, Star Trek Voyager, and Captain Kathryn Janeway.

Why hadn't she thought of it before? Of *course* this actress would have been in more than the one show. Of course. So now at work Christina clicks on Netflix and signs up to the monthly subscription. Tells herself she'll ration the Voyager seasons and not just binge watch them all as fast as she can. Like she wants to. Like Jean said, Christina's been under a rock.

The shows rivet her. That voice. Every time she hears Janeway, she knows she should have guessed she'd grow to sound like that. Just from looking at the black and white's from Ryan's Hope, hearing her on the videos of the old soap clips, she should have known. How could she not?

But Christina doesn't want to find herself like Jean, that hugging herself thing, at the mention of the show. There are 172 episodes to see. She's figured out a system for the whole endeavor. Makes a point of only watching nine episodes a week. One a night and on the weekends, double. Absolutely no more than that. Christina figures four months or so is plenty of time to indulge this little thing she feels. Loves hearing Janeway say: 'Do it.' In that voice.

She has no idea.

It's rare that Christina and Harrison, the two of them, talk like real adults while in the kitchen. Something about little Chrissie, the new cook of the family, remains in the air. That little ghost trying her hardest to feed a poor grieving Harrison, a widower not yet turned twenty-nine.

So tonight, when the rice in the iron frying pan comes out a bit too dry at the edges and hard to the teeth, Harrison joshes, "I don't know why I need you."

And Christina, weary from a mind that only sparks when she's watching Voyager episodes, lays her chin down on her arms, on the table and retorts, "I don't know why I stay." And for once it's all *her* talking. The twenty-year-old speaking. Not the little girl. But Harrison misses that. Simply shoves the crunchy rice aside and eats around it.

Danny is back at the door and Christina harbors a moment

of resentment so strong she considers the option of hiring someone to off him, but it passes.

"Hey Danny." She holds onto the door up high, her arm barring entry. "Harrison's out painting."

"Shit."

Danny usually delivers Harrison's stash on set days of the month. A regular-as-clockwork delivery type of guy. *He should wear those brown shorts.* Could be out tossing papers at wet lawns or delivering pizza, stocking shelves of greeting cards at Walgreen's; if he didn't sleep in till 2 o'clock every afternoon. "It's not dope day, is it?" she asks.

"Nah, just wanted to come and round him up for some fun and games over at my place." He waits but she doesn't invite him in like always. He doesn't realize she's asking herself, *'What would Janeway do to handle this piece of scum?'* Danny probably isn't thinking much about Christina at all, his thoughts focused all in the pocket of his vest.

So he leans back on his heels and takes a long, bored look up one end and down the other length of Heil Avenue. No Harrison on either horizon. Danny exhales, his shoulders round and a paunch leaking over his belt and stretching the black '*Pinche 12 steps*' t-shirt he's tucked in tight.

She waits. Doesn't take her hand from the door. So Danny gives in, shaking his keys. "Well," turning back to his truck and over his shoulder, as he walks away across the lawn, asks, "Do me a favor will you, youngster?" he's turned now, a few little steps backwards as he goes. She hopes he trips on a sprinkler head, *and breaks his skull.*

"Tell him I got a bombita with his name on it." Pats at his vest pocket, like a taunt, reaches his truck; it's parked going the wrong direction on the street. He smiles and gets in.

"'Kay." She counts to ten after he sets his truck in gear. Makes sure to wave at him going, before she shuts the door. *Bastard.*

Harrison sets his easel down in the kitchen and leans into the fridge; humming an old song about a delta lady. Paint streaks his shorts and a smile paints his face.

"Hey baby. Great day. Spectacular day." He dances a little jig, a beer in his hand. "Some of these are maybe good enough to sell. C'mere." He twists off the beer top and takes a swig. "No. Wait, go do something," a hand shoos her out of the kitchen, "I'll set up a show. Gimme a second. Scat."

He calls her back in and there are five canvases on the four chairs and the counter by the toaster. And Harrison's right. These are dammed good.

She's got no idea how he's done it but the perception and depths are stunning. The faraway of the mountains and the closeness of a sage bush and the mid ranges of scurrying jackrabbits all meld like nothing she's ever seen before. The desert winds seem to be blowing in this one on the counter. She feels like she can smell the creosote.

"Wow." Can't think of anything else to say. *How could anyone catch the wind like this?*

He points to another one, a sunset. He's turned the desert floor into some type of rolling ocean. Tinted the bumpy clouds above in a mackerel sky with hints of plum and ginger and lemon and two shades of grays that are there if she looks close enough, but hidden at the same time. And it looks *alive*: like paint wasn't used, but instead, he'd found a way to work in light.

She doesn't have the heart to tell him Danny came by, but the phone rings and Christina doesn't have to.

Chapter Six

CHRISTINA'S OUT OF there before Harrison gets off the phone. But she figures Willis had seen too much of her lately and she rides her bike over to Gina's place instead.

Gina's apartment is crammed full of little girl's dolls and dishes and a lot of high decibel screaming, none of which come directly from Gina herself, but from her three daughters. Jena, Sara, and Terri. It seemed nothing belonged to any one of them and that seemed to be the solution and the problem at the same time. Hence all the yelling.

Gina even says their names in one breath, seven quick syllables. Meaning: *all of you are gonna get it, JenaSaraAnTerri*, as she hands out swats as easily as hugs. "My three gold nuggets."

Christina jokes, "Sounds like a newscasters name "Ginasara Anterre." She intones, "News at six by the valley's most trusted name in network news."

And Gina adds, "More like: Eyewitness coverage of the

disaster in five. Stay tuned." But she smiles the whole time she complains. Gina laughs, pointing a thumb back at the apartment door, as she grinds out her cigarette on the stair's banister, "Any one of these hooligans can feel free to swipe that name and make herself a star."

She and Christina sit out on the steps in front of her door. There's no smoking allowed in the house, and Gina confessed once at work that the only reason she made the rule was to give herself a full ten minutes alone.

"I take maybe five puffs out here. And just that fast the door's cracked open and Terri, the baby always goes, "Mama, why you not gonna come back now?""

I go, 'Lemme get all the smoke outta my lungs first, babygirl.' Man, these children have turned me into a lightweight. I'm a five-puff smoker now. Shit. Try to finish off a stick and I'd get lightheaded."

"At least that's all you're into." Christina leaves it at that. She hasn't come here just to bitch about Harrison. Part of her really does miss talking to Gina.

But Gina sees through that. She coughs and waits in the silence. Probably figured whatever it is, it'll come up before the visit is over. Christina wants to change the subject, when Gina asks, "You still liking all that Star Trek stuff?"

"Oh yeah."

Gina lets Terri and then Jena come out. Terri aims right for Christina's lap, her little hands on Christina's face in the crawling up action. "I'm enjoying the heck out of it."

"I kiss dogs." Her lap-sitter contributes to the conversation. Smiles when Christina looks suitably shocked. Gina counts heads and asks the older one, "Where's your sister?" And the baby scrabbles down. "Me. I get her!"

Christina just thinks, *what would I do without normal people like Willis and Gina?*

"I figured something out last night." Harrison says. His eyes are bright this morning, and not from the dope. He taps his fingers on the kitchen table. "The Van." he says. Waits. But Christina doesn't get it. His smile grows, he'll be patient.

"Ye-eah…?"

"I had a dream. A wonderful one. Your Mom. But it wasn't scary at all. Lots of good light. No shadows. No animals needing rescue. No floods."

Small pets in despair and too much water. Two of Harrison's nighttime antagonists.

"The Van," he repeats. "I'm gonna finish fixing it up and then it's yours. You need to get on the road, girl. I saw it all."

Christina moves so fast from the table she nearly pushes it over. Her temples pound and for a second it feels like she'll drop and seizure right there in the kitchen.

"No fuckin' way," is all that comes to her. And Harrison, filled with the light of his dream, doesn't make out she isn't being rhetorical.

"Yeah. Cool, huh?" he smiles, rapping out a beat with his fingers: da-da-da-ta-da-DA! "I could do it full time, now that the house payment's covered. It's a cherry ride, you know that."

She can't feel her feet. Has to sit down again before she

falls. "Harrison, I can't drive."

"Well." His enthusiasm stops for a second, curbed. He makes actual eye contact with Christina and falters—the thrumming finger-drumrolls petering out. "—yeah, well." And Christina's eyes overflow watching him struggle with that one. Suddenly hating herself for being the one to raise the point.

She looks over her list, for something that might be shiny enough to catch Harrison's attention and drag it away from the idea of her and The Van. But she sees she's been kind of selfish. Her list holds only the house payoff and the art stuff for Harrison. Of the other twenty-three items, fourteen of them are things for her to do and eight are things to buy. If she ever gets around to those. *Should I add another item? One just for Harrison?*

The dread of superstition takes hold of her shoulder and squeezes. No. No changes to the list. She'll have to think of some other way to get him back indoors and away from that damned van.

"Wings and Roots, baby." Harrison thumps the side of The Van. "That's what everybody should be issued from day one." He drops a socket wrench into the open toolbox with a *clang* and pulls a rag from his back pocket. After wiping his hands, then his neck, Harrison reaches for the beer

Christina's brought out. "No roots and you got nothing to tie us to the people who love us here on the ground That's your mom." He drinks like it's the only beer for the next four years. He toasts his lost love: "Time's up. She had to go."

Christina nods. Yep, that's how it is. Time to go. No matter who's here waiting. Harrison's head bobs up, down, to the Van Halen blasting from the patio speakers. His eyes still full with Vivienne, still full of that sorrow. "See you next life. I promise. And that was it. You and me—not enough— she had to go." There's something about this junky old van that sets him talking about things.

They walk back through the scraggly grass to sit in the shade under the patio's awning. "Then there's me. All roots. All the time. No wings to speak of. Rootbound if you wanna be truthful. Can't move an inch in any good direction. I'm so fixed in where I got set down this time around. Shit for luck. Shit for goals. Shit. And more shit."

"Jeez. Cut yourself some slack." Christina realizes this is who'll be teaching her to drive. God.

What else can she say? '*What about me?*' This isn't about anybody but Harrison. Nothing to say to get him to look right at her and focus. His eyes are only for The Van. Nothing to make him see she really means it if she does ask. He isn't hearing her anyway. This is some inside ramble that's got out. Not for her, really. The work he does with his hands leaves his mind free for too many other things.

"But you, baby. You can have both. I'm gonna see to that. If nothing else, you'll get those from us. Roots *and* wings, I promise." He finishes the beer in another two swallows, sits back and knocks out a beat with the empty bottle against his chest: Van Halen lyrics plugging in some vow he's following.

He stands up for a good back un-kinking stretch. And they hear a loud *pop*. His hand shifts to the lower part of his spine. "Whoa. Am I getting old or what?" But he doesn't wait on an answer, kind or not. Harrison only hums and heads back out to toil in the sun. All for her.

And then the driving lessons begin. It's the blind spots that are such a drag. The steering wheel she's pretty much got down. Christina'd been watching Harrison and various bus drivers maneuver vehicles her entire life. What else are passengers supposed to do? So no, the steering wheel isn't the problem. It's the damn blind spots and, well, Harrison too. Maybe a bigger problem than even the blind spots.

"It's okay. No prob. Hell, a little ding. No biggie. Not like I ain't got some on this old truck myself, right?" He's laughing and way too high to be teaching anyone anything. Christina's back hurts. She's got herself in such a state of rigidity. Gripping the wheel the way she'd like to grip Harrison's throat about now.

In anger she says some pretty shitty things. Having to do with operator responsibility. Drug use. And maybe hiring a driving school guy for something so damn important. Harrison blinks. The smile slides from his face; a deflation she can actually chart as it takes place before her eyes.

"Yeah. Well. Maybe…"

Shit.

Christina's out on the bike. She finds her way to the BBQ shop and she and Willis close up the place together, talking about stuff. She's finally told Willis about the win. Not the payout amount, just about the win. Tells him, "I probably can take a year off of work." And leaves the lie at that. She knows it won't be a hard secret to hold. Like his spice combination, a secret's a secret between them. It's not like she's won it and now wants to go back to sleeping on his extra sofa.

The only problem now is that she's asked for half portions of both the spicy fries and the cobbler. And won't eat more even if Willis loads up on the regular sized serving. He just hates that. When Christina asks for a box for half the meat he damn near cries.

She tries changing the subject. Talks about the win. Asks him what he'd do if it was him. Him with the luck. Willis' eyes glisten, "Man, what I'd do? Wooo boy."

She prompts, "What? Open another shop?" Wanting to know what would be on *his* list. Wondering aloud if he could get up farther than twenty-five items to wish on

"Hell no. One would be enough. Wish I mean." Willis laughs at her, "I'd shut this place down or give it all off to my son in-law, Nah, just need the one item. I'd get me a new cat, like ol' Dookie. Remember that cat?"

He looks to the back door, Dookie's wide orange face no longer at the screen, patient. Waiting for scraps. Three years now since that cat'd run off.

"Yes boy, get me a new cat looked like ol' Dookie, and

we'd just spend all my days writing a novel." He rises when someone knocks at the locked front door. It's someone he knows, and he's never been averse to dishing up one more box of take-out.

Willis, he's a touch slower in his step than he used to be, back then, when Dookie and he were pals. But still, one big-shouldered guy. Willis slips the box of links out the door, "Microwave that corn bread at high for fifteen seconds only. Don't need no more than that..." Locks the door again, saying, "Oh yeah. One hell of a novel."

Harrison is on some kind of natural high, now that he's left off driving instruction and started back on The Van. Well, that and he's gone and sold one of his paintings to some lady. She saw him at the market, noticed all his gear in the truck bed, the paint in his hair and asked. "Are you famous?"

Harrison laughs when he tells Christina about it, "Said, 'I would be if anyone bought any of these'. And damn if she didn't hand me a card. Right there in the parking lot." So he went and checked her out. Some tiny gallery, downtown. He took in the five pieces he'd finished recently and she wanted them all.

"Used names like Maxfield Parish, like I knew what that meant. What does he sell? I just kept nodding." Harrison confesses, "Had to look it up, it's some guy's name—He does that glaze thing too, I guess." The Art Lady, it ended up that she wanted to see what Harrison could come up with in acrylics. So he'd promised her another set as soon as

The Van was a bit farther along.

Christina sits with him most morning, watches as Harrison fires up his bong and downs his pot of coffee, ready to head out in the back yard and get to work. His breaks and the lunches she makes him, on the days she doesn't need to be at the office, are filled with stories of how he got The Van in the first place:

"Off some drug mules, a married couple. Straddled the border, making runs down through Calexico, and his old lady wanted to head up north, try Humboldt County for a while. God, they were old way back then. Told me, 'Paint's good and there's very little rust. Eight-track works great too.' And that's all I thought mattered at the time. They hooked me up with a bag, and I said I'd take it. The Van, too.

Told me they'd bought it themselves, three years prior, from some guy who bought a house from them. I can still see that day-glow orange sign, big letters in black Marks-a-Lot, ORIGINAL 1979 WESTFALIA! I'd never ever buy anything someone asked two grand for back then."

"Brought it home and god, it reeked of dope. Man, your mom yelled. Remember that? Her shouting, 'You shoulda just bought a jumbo, freakin' doghouse. Great Dane sized! Woulda cost way less!'"

"Stupid." Harrison shakes his head, remembering. But there seems to be an edge of pride around that assessment. He sits and lists what it still needs, "I gotta get back to stripping out the interior. Prep the cargo floor and then get on the inside paintwork; wouldn't be right not to do the interior. Then there's getting the floor fitting redone. More to it than it looks. That's for sure."

But his eyes are happy, and his posture a bit taller as he writes out his list of to-dos. "New bellows, the sun's got to the ones on there now. Those'll definitely need replacing, 'cause they're a lost cause the way they are now. Trash."

She takes Willis' advice. And after a few days of deliberating, she speaks to Harrison. Christina is a lot calmer now that Willis and Stella are handling the Driving Ed thing. Christina oblivious to the depth of the sting Harrison feels at being subbed in that department. Harrison. The one guy who's always a paragon of driving safely; even while stoned.

But he leaves that snub behind. There are things to do here, on The Van. He slips instead into 'tips for survival on-the road' mode, for once The Van is up and running: "See, baby, you get yourself a big spaghetti pot with a lid, and a roll of duct tape. Line the pot with a plastic trash bag, load in the water and detergent, and of course your unmentionables.

"Seal the bag off with the tape, set the lid on the whole thing. Set it on the floor in the back. While you're driving from town to town your unmentionables are getting nicely agitated, a sixty-mpg gentle cycle."

Picturing it, Christina has to admit it does sound doable. Washing while driving; town to town.

"Next burg you come to run them through some rinse water and line dry the load once you stop and camp for the evening. When it's not washday the pot holds the roll of plastic bags, the tape, your stash of detergent, and your unmentionables folded clean and tidy. Perfecto."

At breakfast Harrison scares the shit out of Christina by pushing his bong to the side: they both look at it, like it's alive and about to complain about this affront. Harrison lets loose a nervous giggle. He sits back and finishes his cup of coffee. "Funny." His apology to the room in general. "No reason to fire it up." Says, "Time to work on The Van—" Stands to rinse his coffee cup out, too. "Thanks for the muffin, baby."

On weekends when Stella asks for helpers for some of the larger projects, Daniel and Christina both volunteer. It's mostly more Excel work. Loading lists into forms. Mindless work, data entry. Stella lets them use their own laptops so they sit in Conference Room B and play Voyager while they work.

Daniel's a fun guy when Denise isn't in the mix. They get along just great; talk about his degree, her new bike. He sees how she named it, asks, "So what type of shipper are you?"

She doesn't know how to answer, but takes a stab,

saying, "Intrepid class all the way." Daniel's eyes crinkle up and he lets out a high cackle. Nearly spits his soda over nachos that Stella's provided as fuel. "Nah. Nah, I mean which combo of relationships do you, uh, favor, uh, among the crew?"

Stella chooses that moment to pop her head in the doorway, "Subs, pizza, or barbeque, folks?" And Christina suggests Willis' place. Stella gives them the thumbs-up sign and leaves them to it again.

Christina glances up to the big teleconference screen. The ex-Borg, Seven of Nine is playing a game of Velocity with the ship's Captain on the holodeck. Like squash, but with phasers and some zooming target thing to shoot at. Both women out of uniform and in work-out clothes. Red for the Capitan. Black for the ex-Borg.

Christina just stares, waiting. *This'll all make sense in a second*, she's sure. Her fingers keep clacking on the keys. Then it comes: Daniel stops typing. Red-faced and looking everywhere but in her direction, he explains, "See, there's Janeway and Chakotay, that's a J/C. B'Elanna and Paris, B/P, Tuvok and um, Neelix. You know—Shipper. What relation-*ship* combo do you like best?"

Ah...

Chapter Seven

AH. CHRISTINA'S GOT it now. Stops typing, and instead looks up to the TV screen again. Daniel waves to the Velocity game; Janeway snapping a towel at Seven's lanky frame, adds, "Janeway and Seven… you know, J/7?"

And it clicks.

He goes on talking, but all Christina hears is an echoing of realization: *Oh. My. God.*

First it's just the YouTube videos. She invites Daniel to her house and he spends that whole Sunday educating her. Daniel seems like a Bedouin with his own likeminded tribe, slash honor codes, and traditional systems of what's Trek canon and what's not. A hierarchy of loyalties. He shows Christina the trackless YouTube dessert like he was the guy who'd built the damn thing.

Slash being the / symbol between two character names. The things people come up with. Daniel, he seemed partial to House/Wilson and she can see why, that scamp House.

But the J/7 videos, *vids* Daniel calls them, were too— too—Christina doesn't even have the words. First discovering the series and now these. All she knows is this YouTube slash thing is a whole new carnival ride. If he hadn't had his heart set on Marc the novelist, she'd have kissed Daniel full on the lips.

Weeks later Christina invites Denise, Jean, Marc and Daniel out to get BBQ, her treat. She's upped her intake of the Voyager episodes now that there's YouTube and slash. And she wants to talk about YouTube videos. Willis brings out the sookie for them all—one huge cookie warmed up and loaded with scoops of vanilla ice cream.

Willis sets it in the middle of the table and hands out spoons and new checkered napkins. The group, groaning in unison, offers smiles all around. A suitable noise considering the ribs they've just put away. But just the same, everyone grabs a spoon… even Christina.

"Won't he kick us out soon?" Jean asks, the first to break down and dig in. "Ummmmm."

Christina takes a spoonful, knowing Willis is watching. "I'm pretty sure the only reason he'll want us to move is to help take out the trash just before he locks up."

Christina hasn't come right out and said, 'I'm watching J/7 vids.' She uses the word *Voyager*. Doesn't know how Jean might react to the virtual violation of her cherished Mary Ryan. So in her heart she silently thanks Marc when he puts things so delicately, asking "So Tina, how do you like the little community you've fallen into?"

"I cannot get over how great these vids are. Do you know how they make them? Can anyone do it?"

"I guess so. That's why it's called *You*Tube."

Denise said, "It's all done on Windows Movie Maker. If you've got Windows on your machine, there you go."

News to Christina. "Really?" she rears back and sets her spoon down. "How about if you have a Mac?"

"Oh yeah. Use iMovie. My brother-in-law, sells rugs and draperies? He made his own commercial for nearly nothing and they copied it over to the cable station? So they could play it on rotation."

Who knew?

Denise wants to know what song Christina'll use for her first one, "If you make one, I mean?"

Christina sits back. "Don't know." The others wait. "I don't know enough about it yet." Jean's spoon dips into the sookie again. "Who to ask. All the possibilities." Christina taps her forehead, once, lightly; not ready to wake anything just yet. "All the questions."

Daniel bumps shoulders with Marc, adds, all sweetness and light, "I guess she could find one of the shipper forums…"

Christina keys *Wiki* and *Voyager* and *Shipper* into a Google search. This brings up links to cruise lines and Voyager summaries for episodes called Juggernaut and Eye of the Needle (which she bookmarks for later, to read and see if she's missed nuances once she's watched all of the seasons). She's upped all the episode watching to as many episodes she can watch on Netflix at one go before she's too tired to take more in.

Basically, the win's made her more than jumpy, and this compulsion is only growing. Now she's searched out Janeway/Seven videos on YouTube. Adding to her Favorites list, rating the ones she laughed at. Posting comments when she's truly felt moved by a few of the vidder's work.

This's something I could do. She thinks. Being diligent in reading the info blurb as each vid played. And out of the corner of her eye, as the credits roll, she sees it. *Hey Shippers! Check out my Ready Room for more J/7 fun.* Humm. Ready for any *Janeway* and *J/7*, she holds her breath and clicks on the *Ready Room* link.

Bingo. A forum.

Christina hates logging out of The Captain's Ready Room forum she's found. She loves the bold look of the site's deep reds and glossy blacks and grays. Seven's eyepiece embossed on a plump shiny heart, snug in the heart's curve up to the right. And the captain's four pips, gleaming golden down on the left, strung along to heart's lower point. A perfect balance. A lacy black script at the glossy red core: *Talk Nerdy to Me.*

Every time she logs in that wonderful Janeway voice comes up growling "In the Ready Room!" She considers joining instead of only logging in as a guest. Studies the screen name she's decided on. Likes it somewhat, but not totally. She launches up the forum and signs up, with the username TulipAna. Having an online personality feels more real than herself, somehow.

First, she only lurks. Sets herself the task of reading all the other posts as far back as they go, starting with the threads that grab her attention first. Thorough. Methodical. A new notebook keeps a list of the threads she's covered, so there'll be no wasted motions. There's a *lot* of reading to do.

By Friday she's found a section called Archives and, ready, she digs in deep. She jots down any lingo for reference later. Watches as members wax and wane in their participations.

If she likes someone's posts, if they're funny or have a way with words, she checks their member info. Ponders about unchecking the checkbox in her profile that reads: Hide email address from public?

The people using the forums are lively, having fun; their banter mostly light and comic. And though Christina joins to find out about making videos, the sheer world-sized-ness of it all pulls her in. But it leaves her mute when it comes to joining in on their banter.

The flirting, first of all, seems outrageous, frequent, and for the most part, playful. She's talked with Daniel about it.

He seems to think it's no big woo, "You've seen the cartoons haven't you, the dog sitting at the computer talking to the cat? And the punchline is, 'Online, no one knows you're dog'."

Christina wants him to explain some of the jargon. Then asks, "So wait, is lurking good or bad? I still don't get it." It's all quite an education. Jean watches and grins every time Daniel and Christina sit in the break room and discuss all this.

But after reading all of the forum's archive pages, going several years back, Christina realizes these folks probably have never set eyes on one another. Yet stranger's they weren't.

She reads and reads and thinks, *Plenty of possible friend material.* But she's not jumping right in just yet. She finds herself sneaking looks at the board's calendar, feeling guilty as she does. Like she'd be caught edging towards stalking, but then she tells herself, *it's just to see whose birthdays are in which month.* There's crAZy4J7. She hasn't added her age to her profile, but from her posts Christina figures that they might be about the same age. This one used gestures or comments enclosed in asterisks for all of her posts. *Either that or it's an old guy who thinks some girls express themselves that way.*

And there's Nomad07, she seems older, maybe a worrier type, a droll sense of humor that's for sure. Her avatar is a silhouette of a runner. Sleek. Christina pictured Nomad07 to be thin, lanky. Spare in shape like her posts are. Maybe this one could be a friend.

But the gigantic find here is that folks are writing fan

fiction. For J/7 Shippers. A combative pair of Klingons post an awful lot, Klingon_1 and Klingon_2, they put up the best stuff. Folks post responses that shower these two with praise. Begging for new installments. But they're just two of a long list. Everybody here, it seems, writes. At first, Christina thinks the Klingons might both be the same person, but their fan fic styles are too wide apart to be coming from one brain. No one can argue with themselves like these two.

Another pair are Kirigami and ITV. These two are vidders and ITV creates something called 'alts'. ITV, like one of the Klingons, lives in Bakersfield, her profile says. They must be two of the forum's first members because their post count stats were ginormous. Kirigami's capacity for a long whinge can be a bit entertaining, and ITV mentions the lack of things to do in town more than a little bit.

crAZy4J7's way with asterisk abuse makes Christina crack up to no end. First Christina takes it for granted, no guys on the forum (or 'The Board' as they call it, like Harrison says The Van). Turns out, no. Nearly every assumption is wrong. Young, old, male, female. When she checks profiles and birthdays, and reads back along the various threads, spotting the things that they chat about, every mental picture she's painted seems wide of its mark, and completely, utterly wrong in some cases. Nearly all her assumptions just from the poster's avatars are off in some important way. But maybe that's the fun of being here. Like Daniel's comic strip of a puppy at a keyboard, grinning and telling that nearby cat *"On the internet, no one knows I'm a dog."* Christina thinks that's a good way to look at things and she sets about searching Google images; trying to find a picture of a suitably Trek-looking puppy to use as her own avatar.

She visits the site daily. Loves seeing her TulipAna in the *Users Online* section at the bottom of the page. 'But no one knows I've come to visit', she tells herself, 'What can it hurt?' Christina stays on the board for hours and only her dry eyes remind her to take a break.

It's a new world after a long captivity, like she's braved escape from that faked life at the Outlook. Wandered on her own all night long and now it's morning. Christina, no, *TulipAna*, feels like she's finally hacked through a jungle, and come upon the village she must have been kidnapped from at birth. She's found a tribe who have the same eyes she does. It makes her feel like she exists somewhere for once, so absolutely real.

Game threads, chat threads, threads devoted to the ex-Borg Seven of Nine and ones set up solely for all things Captain Janeway. Some having nothing at all to do with Voyager or this particular pairing. And pictures galore, oh my. Yes. Some posts are alterations; an entire thread called *Alter-ations*. ITV from Bakersfield is the star here. Her work, ALTS she calls them, are fantastic. It's a whole world of its own.

Christina browses the topic called The Suggestion Box. It's a place for members to pose problems that the others can then offer advice for. A little village devoted to the care and feeding of fellow shippers. It takes quite a few pages of back posts to realize not all members take it too seriously.

ITV: I've always wondered about Klingon pubic grooming…

Klingon_2: Well, ITV…if someone has to wonder it might as well be you.

****

crAZy4J7: How can I keep my parents out of my hair? *Why.Oh.Why.Me???*

LemonSkye: talk to a Klingon, I hear they're big on grooming advice.

****

LargeMarge: I think I'm ready. How should I come out to my boss at work?

FaeLight07: LM, Hooray for you, girl! Send me a personal message or your email, we'll talk.

This is where she comes out of hiding and makes her first contact on the board. She takes a long afternoon composing the post, writing it over and over until she thinks it's brief enough. Wishes she knew how to make it funny. Shies away from using any asterisks.

TulipAna: My dad wants me to take the camper van he's repairing and take myself on an extended road trip. But I'm not sure I want to go. What should I do?

Klingon#1: Who's buying the gas?

crAZy4J7: Life sux + then I come home to find the new puppy's chewed up one of my better slingbacks. *Shakes Head. Always.Something*

Klingon_1: Who are you? And what have you done with TulipAna?

****

Christina checks back on the thread all that day, to see if anyone else replies. She's hoping that FaeLight07 might.

At home Harrison's still on his riff about how the history of the thing is what matters most. The gem of the fact that there are parts for The Van, even now, this many years after they stopped production in 2003, "The love of the vehicle." he lectures. "Car groups still getting together for this baby." Sliding his hands along the gray Bondo.

Softly, Harrison takes her hand. "Chrissie, c'mer." He whispers, "close your eyes," runs her hand in his along the smooth side of the van, "Feel that?"

There's just the slightest touch of graininess running under her fingers; if her eyes were open she doesn't think she'd be able to detect it in the sun. But Christina nods. "Uh-huh." Opens her eyes, back to the brightness of the day, the brightness of his smile. Harrison promises: "I'm gonna get that out for you."

She's staring again at the one item on the list:

No.5 Cut hair.

Thinks maybe she can replace it with Learn to Drive. But Nicky, on her lap, looks up at her, as if he's reading along, and has her number. Even he knows it's a cop out.

But shit. Harrison's got his Bondo, and Danny sniffing around, and enough grief with Christina not spencing her winnings as it is.

Yeah. It's all about Harrison. Right. Who's Christina kidding?

Chapter Eight

"TOO BAD IT'S the model with the bay window instead of the split screen style, boy were those cherry."

Harrison's gotten a huge amount of work done so far. He's even attached the 'pop up' top with the tent thing in it; dark green and cream-stripped canvas. "You mind if I use some of the money? Get some tools I don't got now? Keeps me from asking Danny… Though I'll probably ask him to help when I get around to yanking the engine."

Dinners still full of talk about chassis plate locations and M-Code formats. Where they stamped the body number, "Behind the front seat on the early nineteen fifty-eight, pre-October models," he adds, like that's a big thing to know. He leans away from his plate and hunches over some diagram for the wiring key. Harrison shifts his plate away and goes online, looking for a new fuse box, each of their new laptops sit in as two dinner guests at the table each night.

"Gonna do this up right," he promises, sitting forward in his recliner after dinner, papers all around him, ignoring his beer. The list grows a bit longer; morphs into one for a trip once it's running, more than for fixing The Van:

Portable chemical toilet. "No." She says. "Just. No, Harrison."

A camping stove, storage box, "Matches the interior," he assures. Harrison's thought of everything. Various camping equipment, "You need a deep Dutch oven if you wanna keep on baking your muffins. Attachable stand-alone tent." He mutters, like some magical incantation, "Attachable side awnings."

Checks off the things he's got done so far: Air conditioning, transmission, water pump, rear swing table, shocks. "We can spring for a GPS now. No prob, if you wanna go that route. Mount it on that small map table on your dash."

She jokes, "Whose trip is this?" and he nearly tears up as he draws a line through that one, shaking his head reluctantly as he acquiesces. Harrison crosses more and more niceties off his list.

The days she's sick of all The Van talk she ribs Harrison, joking under a layer of her true feelings. Tells him, "I'd be just as happy with a squareback, yellow, a Type-3. I'd even learn to drive stick for one of those." and Harrison just grins and grins, he's got her now—she's been checking out the websites.

The days she hates most are when Danny shows up with tools that Harrison needs. If she comes home and his car is out front, she just keeps on pedaling. And most times that's a lot of extra miles.

The scale reads 158. She's on her bike all the time now; she likes the feeling of the wind against her face, washing Danny's laugh from her living room, from her mind. Even with no place to go, Christina's glad for the hard, downward push with her thighs, the feel of her biceps with each pull up at every revolution's cycle. She purposely keeps the tension at a high level. Hated how the clerk guy at the shop, back where they took it to add decals, took a quick look at her, then advised her to keep the gears on low.

She's got no idea how much she's needed back at home. How hard it is for Harrison to keep saying 'Nah, man. No thanks,' to Danny.

"Here's my new rules—for me—Harrison. No one else." Danny's with him. sitting on the patio late one evening. Christina's bedroom window is cracked open for some air. Their voices waft in, like smoke. Harrison's voice over her head, "I go to bed every night. Maybe at ten, maybe at two. But I shower, stay stripped to my boxers, and slip into bed. Under covers, light out. Stereo on low."

Danny shifts in his chair, on auto pilot. Can't change the channel though he's probably itching to. He's seen this one too many times. "When I wake up—the first time, son, none of this rolling over shit and hitting the internal snooze button. When I wake up, I get straight out of bed Get dressed. If I'm dressed, then no lying down again. See what I'm getting at here? Routine."

Danny breaks in, "Sounds like prison, man." His tapping on the table comes in through her window, too. And Christina knows he's laid out his outfit, the syringes all nice and ready. Empty now, just waiting for 'yeah' from Harrison.

"Well then if that's what gonna keep me on the straight. Routine. Then that's where I'll put myself."

"Shit." A dismissal. The wondering about balls goes unsaid.

"Breakfast." Harrison continues, "Clean out the cat's box. Okay, maybe a hit, maybe two. But nowhere near like before. Then it's The Van. The Van till lunch. Then after that, more of The Van."

"Yeah, well—"

But Harrison cuts him off, "—Chrissie's home by then, and it's dinner. Still light out? Then more of The Van. Gets dark? Then it's time on the laptop or with the painting. That's my life. And as you may 'a noticed, going to your place for an evening of piss, snot, and drool is not on that list. And it won't help you bringing it here, neither."

She can hear the zipper closing, for transport to someone's house who is still in need and willing to give in to Danny's generosity. Danny hauls himself out of the too-tight folding chair, done with this inhospitable crap. Danny tells Harrison: *Pussy.*

Christina bikes and bikes. Nowhere to go and nowhere to be. Her world reduced to the sun, this road, and the spinning of the chain and gears. She stands, really gets going. Heads for the other side of town. Just because she can.

On Heber, she sees the *For Rent* sign for the first time. A tiny old-fashioned plaza. Looks like maybe six shops in a U on the ground floor and some apartments up top. The rent sign is for an apartment. *Humm.*

Chapter Nine

I T COMES TO Christina a bit at a time. But she's finally able to put this into words: Harrison knows that The Van is something he's got to do. For himself as well as her. He can't let go of this task or he'll be letting go of too much. At thirty-seven he's got a job he doesn't need anymore, a mortgage he's no longer responsible for, and a daughter who, until now, hasn't been aware that he knows for sure if he gets this done for her the bad dreams will end. Prophetic dreams. Haunting him in oblique ways. He wakes up screaming too often. She can hear him from her room even with both their doors shut. And in the mornings, there's always that hint that most of the images haven't faded totally, as Harrison's eyes focus on the reality of the kitchen.

She heard him once, out on the patio, confessing to some friend from the bar, *Viv on the stairs, though we've never lived anywhere with a second floor. But there she is, a cadaver, not beautiful like all my other dreams. But not scary.*

Heading upstairs, 'You coming or what?' she wants to know. Me, who never had somewhere to go or somewhere to be, except with Viv. And the water around my feet just climbing higher and higher.

Harrison can't fuck this one up. It's obvious he's battling that 'place to be'.

Christina makes a pact with herself, as she pedals past the *For Rent* sign, accidentally on purpose, for the fifth time. Promises if she unclenches and gets up the strength for doing a list thing, then Harrison won't make her go out on the road with The Van. She's never heard of magical thinking. Really believes it'll work. Pedals and pedals, her thighs burning as she tries coming up with something less drastic to go with.

Nowadays a twenty-mile ride is nothing for her. The scale shows a drop of forty-five pounds from her starting point of 185. But size-wise she's way down from 1X tops. She takes more of Harrison's t-shirts from his laundry, folds them up and slips them into her own dresser drawers. She's not complaining. Not at all.

On the J/7 board life, she's even graduated to one-on-one DMs. One of her new friends lives up in Arcadia so the time zones were compatible.

TulipAna: I'd never say this on the board but I'm getting so steamed with all the drama. Like all those astericks. Jeez. Am I wrong?

ARCoBAL: I always go with a live and let live approach.

Squint through all the outrageous stuff. Ignore members that set you off. Skip any posts entirely that you know you just can't hang with reading. The high road—that's my road.

TulipAna: Yeah. I guess so, I don't want to step on any toes when it comes to the group.

****

ARCoBAL: So when were you going to come out for a RL visit?

TulipAna: soon… never… later. now.

ARCoBAL: Do I get to pick one of those?

TulipAna: I don't know. I guess I could.

ARCoBAL: Well think on it. The door's always open. It's just me and my sister here, so… Besides, you're close enough.

TulipAna: How will I know I'm up for it?

ARCoBAL: 'Now' is always easy to recognize. You'll know.

They're back home one night from being out for dinner and Christina trips stepping out of the truck. "You okay?" Harrison comes around to her side and looks at the concrete, "What was it?"

"Me." she yanks up on her jeans. "These're getting too loose."

"You need to get some stuff that fits."

"I'm okay."

He unlocks the front door. "Nah. You should go online.

See about some new tops and jeans." He hasn't been blind to how many of his embezzled T-shirts show up on Christina's thinner frame lately.

"It's not time yet."

"Sure it is. You're tripping now." He moves to his laptop. If she won't do it, he will. "It's time."

"No. I mean, I'm still losing." she grabs her midsection. Looks plenty small to Harrison and he says so. But Christina's adamant. "I'll get some things later, when I get down into the next size. I promise."

Harrison's in some good mood again. He's still crowing. "Sold another one." That was why they were out to dinner. This one canvas went for even more than the first. He's selling these, like, one every month. On a roll. She wants to say: *Good for you.* But doesn't. Lets the chance pass and her regret at doing so mounts. Until they grow too big to wrestle into smaller manageable deeds. Uncomplicated smiles. Simple moments when she's truly listening as he's talking to her. Straightforward breaths that aren't dragging some unspoken comment in and out with them.

Instead, she holds on to it all. Accruing pressure, the way she lets the savings accounts grow. The way she won't do nice things for herself. Like the win never happened. Like she's still not worthy, so it's all the more difficult to let anyone else be worthy either.

Pounding on her. That's what it feels like, all of Harrison's soaringly good ideas and his spectacular plummets. Pounding. Like now, suddenly, she's responsible for being some better, smarter, quicker, happier person, to balance all his shit. Instead of the truth—all that green is no eraser for her mistakes-to-date.

"You oughta come and see the corner they gave me to display the stuff, I got it set up real nice."

"Yeah. I could do that." *Say anything. What's it matter?*

Danny's got his back up against the van's open side door, regaling Harrison with old repeated tales of their past drug days. Priming the pump, so to speak. "God, 'member that one chick from Indio, she—"

"Oh, Mother of God." Harrison can't believe it. "Mother fucker, sonofabitch."

Danny laughs, "What?" and inclines his head into The Van's cab. Harrison is on his back with one arm over his eyes.

He's broken the odometer. Harrison shifts, rubs one eye with his little finger, grips his wrench tighter, then knocks it on his head, cusses once more, and whispers. "I cannot fuckin' believe I just did that." He keeps his eyes from meeting Christina's. And she keeps silent, as if that helps her not witness it. He wiggles out from under the steering wheel and sighs. "Fuck."

Sits up, hangs his head. Danny reaches into the cooler he's carried from his place and walks around The Van to his stricken buddy. Bangs a beer on Harrison's shoulder, "C'mon. It's too damn sunny to cry out here. Let's go sit." Leads the way to the patio and as he calls them, 'those damned skinny chairs.' Steering Harrison with one hand on his shoulder. "Tell mama."

"I was trying to reset the odometer. I busted the fucker."

"Ah. Bummer."

"Fuck." Harrison's neck cracks as he lowers his forehead into his palm. Danny can hear it loud and clear. Christina hunkers in her seat, still not saying anything.

"Umm-hum. Now what?"

"Shit."

"You mentioned that. Once or twice."

Harrison stands. Slides the patio door open and heads to the kitchen for his bong.

Now that he's got a bit of a buzz, he's figured it out, aloud, "All's not lost."

Danny takes the last swig from his current bottle, then tosses the empty back into the melted ice. "What a fuck-up pair we make, huh?"

Harrison sits a bit taller in his patio chair. Not having any of it. He's talked himself out of the shits and can see daylight after all. "I can fix it. Sure. Nothing's a lost case until you lose it. Right, Chrissie?"

She just says, "Talk to Danny. He says you guys're both alike."

"Bullshit." Harrison says, "We're miles apart. And what's that got to do with The Van anyway?"

"Bullshit," comes Danny's retort, "We're practically twins."

"My ass."

"We're both rats, boy. Get over yourself."

At that Christina gets up and goes through the patio door, pulling it only mostly-closed behind her so their debate is still heard.

Harrison tilts his head to the kitchen. "I raised her. Didn't find some relative and drop her off some morning. I'm no rodent. Didn't take the truck and scram. I'm still here. I got a routine. Still doing it right. What you got goin', real-life wise?"

"Sure, Harrison." Danny gives him that one, but lifts his last beer from the cooler, loosens one finger from its neck and aims, jabs, "But just remember, son, my point here is: without the youngster here, you'd be just another user and abuser like your pal Bud here." Points to his own chest. Thumps once. "Maybe not breaking things you can afford to get new, but with no van to fix or bust." Takes a swig, finger now heavenward. "Just like ol' Danny boy. Living life by the gram, and not much else."

"Don't shit me, son," is all Harrison can give back.

"Don't shit *me*, Harrison. You're the same grade of crap I am. No different rodent except for the part of town we found to burrow into." Danny shades his eyes and burps, shifts in the patio chair, a thumb back to the house, "Who d'you think she'd get to be if you were out of the picture, huh?"

It's dark in the house when she comes in from work on Tuesday. Nicky chooses this moment to be velcro-cat, and has to be pushed away from under her feet. She sets her bag down and heads for the kitchen. Looks for a note on the table. But no. Glances back out at the yard, but he's not there either. It's got to be nearly 8 o'clock.

She reaches for the light switch and, for a second, the new brightness in the kitchen is painful to her eyes. Nicky twines, a figure eight, begs: *pick me up*—"Barrr-wrooo?"

The clock ticks too loud as she scoops up the fuzzy body, "Where's Harrison, Nick?" She heads back into the darkness of the living room.

Drops the cat and clutches at the kitchen's doorframe. Nicky runs for the closet. Harrison is still as stone. Slumped in his recliner, legs sprawled, eyes at half-mast.

"Fuck Me, Harrison. You scared the shit out of me."

She wants to go hit him. Get a rise out of him, like he'd just done to her. "Harrison?"

The need to get closer shifts. Converts to fear. Something's not right. She knows she should go check his pulse. Asks one more time, a higher tone out of her mouth. "Harrison? You okay?"

He blinks, slurs, "*Viv?*" Or something near it.

Christina doesn't stay and ask. Instead, she heads directly down the dark hallway, a guiding hand trailing the wall to the door to his room where she snatches his comforter off his bed. Stomps back to the recliner.

Pissed now; wants to slap the top of his head off, she's so pissed.

Slows just shy of the big chair. He's slipped down a bit, to his left. She watches, gripping the comforter that's no comfort at all. Harrison can't get a purchase with his hands on the arms of the leather chair.

She hears that sound his throat makes as he struggles, a drugged-out stutter that Christina abhors hearing. Like bat's wings rustling or skittering crawling things. Deep from somewhere inside him. Some dead place he carries; on occasion finding this need to dig down and reclaim it.

Christina hates knowing something must have hit the fan today. But now's not the time to find out what. She steels herself and takes the final step closer to lay the cover across his knees. Pulls it up to his chest and presses it there. To secure it. To check his thumping heart. Turns on the TV and lowers the volume. Harrison can't stand waking up to a quiet room.

She reaches for the little throw pillows on the sofa. Dips to pick up the one on the floor under the coffee table, stuffs each one deep into the chair on both sides so his tilting's corrected. Gentle.

She knows he's too out of it to hear her, but she asks anyway, barely a whisper, the words rising no higher than his shins, "You gonna be okay, Dad?" She's knelt to unlace his shoes.

There's a huge thump and Christina's being shaken so hard that she opens her eyes with a cry and tries to sit up. Thinks it's an earthquake. That she needs to get to Harrison in the living room. But she's pinned. The shaking is him. "Harrison?"

Harrison's on his knees at the side of her bed. His hand on her shoulder. His head lolling at her pillow. Crying. Cries like she used to hear every night that first year her mom died. Crying like he's going to break right in half from the wracking sobs.

Christina scrambles away to the other side of the bed. This is different. He's still high. She can feel it. She has to get away; bedsheets tangle around her. The crying is mixed with a slackness. An out-of-control spastic feeling in his sobs.

"Viv…" he slurs, and Christina's hand goes to her mouth. Stands, tries stepping to the door and space in the hall.

"Sorry… sorry, baby." He won't stop; he's crawling toward her as she tries to move past him and make her way free. His arms are no good support. He bounces off his chin, falling and rising and falling again. "Really need ya' t'know… for th' begging… so, so sorry."

She throws up right there.

It takes just the one call but by the time she's showered and dressed Stella is out front waiting.

THE SUGGESTION BOX:

TulipAna: What does it take to be Brave?

Fae_light07: Sometimes too much. Sometimes surprisingly little.

TulipAna: Is there a way to start?

ARCoBAL: {{{{TulipAna}}}} Anything we can help with?

TulipAna: Life.

Klingon #1: Oh. That… Well Then, you're up a creek— we know nothing about THAT.

ARCoBAL: Screwed.

FaeLight07: Yep, can't help there—screwed alright... (I'll PM you dearie. Hold on, help's on the way)

"We got six units total up here. It's a real nice, quiet place after the shops close downstairs."

Just from looking up through the green of the big tree in the courtyard at the six units that ring the shops, Christina can see the rental must be minuscule. As they move up the stairs Jeffrey, the guy with the keys, points to his left, "It's that one, number 4. That door and the window on each side. Living room and kitchen." He's got a nice sounding voice. She likes listening to him. He drowns out the guilty yammering going on in her mind.

This upper level is a rectangle, instead of a U like downstairs. The walkway's decorated with wrought-iron railings. Like the French Quarter somewhere east. Units one and two face four and five on the longer ends of the space. Units three and six sit at each of the shorter ends. Window, door, window, and window, door, window, all the way around. Jeffrey jangles his key ring and makes a selection, "Here we go."

"Living room and eating space runs eleven by sixteen feet." He points; it looks like a fat bowling lane to Christina. The kitchen is shorter, the size of postage stamp. Easily a third of her kitchen at home. "Two bedrooms at the back, the slightly smaller one is eleven by ten."

She thinks: *Space to do things from the list.*

"Four rooms and a bath." Jeffrey tosses the keys, left

hand, right, left. Smiles. Waits. The whole place can't be more than 700 square feet if it's an inch. Jeffrey points to the baseboards, says, "You got a cable hook-up here and in the little bedroom, too. And a place to park in back." Christina nods at that; parking in the back, no one would know if she were home or not.

She goes for another peek at that tiny kitchen. "Gas stove," He points to a cream-colored fridge so short Christina can see over its top without raising up on her toes. "Laundry room downstairs. The bar next door." Jeffrey backs out of the kitchen and leads her through the rest of the place. Christina counts a full seven steps down the hallway.

In the larger of the two bedrooms, he opens two narrow French doors, waving at a miniature balcony that faces a drop into an alley. Gestures at the side of the next building, a sooty brick wall. The bar. "View sucks," he admits.

Still, there's enough room for her bike out there on that little balcony. What more can she ask for? She smiles at Jeffrey, and says, "I'll take it," pulling a checkbook from her bike bag, "Three months. No, a half-year in advance if we can keep the rent at seven hundred dollars, not seven-fifty, for thirty months. Okay?"

Jeffrey grins and nods. Only blinks the once. "The bar always gets 'em."

Chapter Ten

HER THOUGHTS ARE on how she can skin out of actually going on the road once The Van is done. The logistics. The toll. Then there's The Apartment. Christina's always been her own girl. Did what she wanted when she wanted. But that girl never acted like such a shit to Harrison.

At home she cooks a meal for him that's been a standard for good times for most of her life. Trying to figure out how she'll tell him she wants to move out. Not that she has to go today. But Christina knows. She *does* have to go.

Fried chicken breasts, green beans and pearl onions sautéed in almonds and garlic, carrots in orange marmalade with nutmeg, and chicken Rice-a-Roni. Harrison takes one look and whispers, "This is either you're not mad at me anymore or The Van. You gonna tell me which?"

Christina can't look him right in the eye, he's still high. Speeding, though she can also smell the bong water. Or else he's on something else to get him straight. Back up to level from that slurry, listing, heroin state. She turns away, reaches into the fridge for the cranberry juice and the iced goblets.

Her mumbles aim into the coolness of the fridge. "Both I guess." *God, what a shit.* "You. And the on-the-road stuff."

And it comes to her. Let Harrison finish The Van and think she's left and gone on the road. Keep the pain of *going*-going from him. Just that easily she finds she can lie to him: "I'm gonna do it."

Harrison comes up behind her, a dumb, happy bear. Twitchy and scratching, looking for a big hug. He takes the pitcher of juice from her and sets it on the table, then dances her around the kitchen. "You won't regret it, babe. It'll be the time of your life. Promise. Start in San Diego, wind your way up the coast to the redwoods. The greatest nine-hundred miles of your life." His hands are trembling; she has to find some reason to pull away.

"And I've got a surprise for you," he says, fiddling with his fork once they're seated. "Wait'll you see. But first let's eat this feast. Looks swell, great. I'm starved. Swear to god— the day I—well… Forget that. We're celebrating, right?" And he sits, grinning, damn near vibrating right off his seat. All the meal long.

His surprise is that he's installed a cassette deck in the van. She stares, not wanting to harsh his mellow in this one. But then Harrison explains: "I kinda sorta fucked up in one area so I thought I'd redeem my sorry ass in another." He comes clean about how serious a broken odometer is, and promises it'll all be fixed. But he's tweeking. Who knows what the effort to fix it all will really end up being?

"Good as new baby, truth. But," he says, "and here's the good part—" Apparently, while he was talking to the guy about a new odometer, the guy asked what type of sound system's in the dash. Harrison spins the story out for her, lots of hand gestures, "'Eight-Track', I say, but told him, that's coming out. I wanna put all my LPs in iTunes and burn a slew of your CDs. For you to take along. And I got to telling him about my collection and how I'm gonna install a killer stereo system for you.

And the guy goes, "you're thinking of one of them In-Dash CD, MP3, WMA Receivers right, iPod 'an Bluetooth ready? Right? Well *Neg-a-tori* my friend.'" Harrison mimics the guy's baritone, "'Wrong. Wrong and wrong. You wanna install a midrange-of-the-mill cassette player. Primo speakers of course.'"

"Of course." Christina echoes, ready to chew her own ears off to shorten this story. She hates whatever type of speed he's on. *Really* hates it.

"Nah, seems with a regular cassette player—and the primo speakers—you can get one of them car cassette adapters for your iPod; looks like a cassette with a rat's tail attached to it, and runs maybe nine bucks each. Works with any type of player with a headphone jack.

The guy tells me, 'get her ten of 'em if you want. Hell. Stock up. One of these in the car ain't nobody's gonna want to rip off your smokin' CD player or you lose your fuckin' unit's remote cause there ain't none. You're behind the times. Yeah, behind like a fox.'" Harrison stops while he pushes another forkful of dinner into his mouth and smiles at her; proud and happy, like he's just discovered penicillin or something.

Christina smiles, nods. Extra drinks of cranberry juice because right now swallowing's impossible without it. The dinner's ashy lumps in her mouth. *Oh yeah. I'm so out of here.*

Harrison stands at Rose's desk, grinning and waggling his fingertips at Christina as she comes from the back of the office. End of shift and he's come to take her out to dinner. His treat, BBQ. He's sold another painting. He's so proud of being somewhat clean and mostly sober for a full two weeks now. Harrison wants to tell Willis and Tonette all about this last big art sale. How well The Van's coming along. If Christina still worked at the Outrage he might be taking out an ad.

"Hey, baby. Ready?"

"This the famous Harrison?" Stella's come from her office and stops, seeing Harrison. "Well, hi there!"

Christina steps over to face them both. Still not ready to have Stella talk to Harrison. "Yep. Here's the guy." Her fake smile pushes her cheekbones up so high it makes her squint. Harrison's no better.

"Howdy." He turns to Christina, "It's the art lady. My first sale."

"Congratulations. Big day, huh?" Stella says. Not a word

about being dragged out of bed to come rescue his daughter at 2 A.M. Presentation is everything.

"Gonna go get BBQ. Celebrate with friends."

"Waldo's? Down near Herber?"

"No. No. The good stuff. Word of Mouth. Only place for BBQ."

Christina takes a breath and decides to unclench. Just let it all go. So she pokes Harrison's midsection. Adds, "He'd know." Thawing just a touch. To Stella, then including Rose too, she asks, "You want to meet us there?"

Stella looks to Harrison. You can see she wants to give the guy a break. He looks so scrubbed and, well, tired. "Sure. Why not?"

Rose drives Stella in her SUV and follows Harrison's truck. At Word of Mouth, heading for the front door, Stella comments, "You sure are one safe driver, Harrison." About to say more, but the lure of the BBQ grabs her and she's rendered speechless for a moment. Harrison just nods, holding the door for the ladies.

At the register, Willis opens his arms wide, comes around the counter, gathers them all in as one bunched group. Hugs even Rose and Stella who he hasn't met yet. Ushers the group to a wide table and before they can shift their rears in the seats to settle, he's back, slapping down a heaped plate of warmed cornbread, a crock of butter, and cutlery setups for each, wrapped in red checkered napkins. Family style, and definitely more cornbread than four diners require considering the portion sizes to come.

There's crooning over the speakers, a guy Harrison says is Francis Dunnery. "Love this song," his hands drumming, Christina just barely hearing it over all the talk. "Willis' big on burning his own CDs." Harrison says to Stella.

Stella stops chewing, listens, then swallows a big gulp of sweet tea, cocks her ear to see if she's got it right, "Too Much Saturn, Not Enough Moon?" Harrison's floored, calls Willis over and they both marvel at Stella's eclectic ear. She gets another bear hug from Willis for that.

Stella says, "You and Christina, you both have the biggest smiles." Willis nods as he refills her mason jar to the brim.

Christina can't figure out what's driving her to do this but she knows it's a freight train. Unstoppable now that it's got going.

Harrison's bong has been a way of life since her childhood, and his going off to Danny's for whatever was just something he did. But now... Now, she thinks she's dragging him toward all this new shit. Speedballs at home and crying jags in her room. Crank at dinner. Then the great turnaround and all this straight and narrow stuff. All on board, no stops till daylight.

It's up to her. She knows that nothing can stop the urge. If she stays at the job, Harrison might see her any day out on the street. And that would ruin everything.

She's on autopilot now. First, to say yes to The Van was

stupid enough. Then to the apartment, and now, sadly, to saying goodbye to Stella and the girls at the office.

So it's *adios* to the crew. No more potlucks, no more Jean and her encyclopedic soap opera knowledge. Goodbye to novelists drinking coffee in the break room, asking one another about story arcs and who they've gotten rejection letters from lately.

God. She's gonna miss these folks.

She acts like she didn't know about the email; subject line: DON'T Show this to TINA!

The biggest surprise is the Voyager theme. She's blushing from the moment they grab her at her desk and she's hustled down the corridor toward the lunchroom. "We mean it, no peeking," Jean warns, guiding her into what must be Conference Room B.

"Okay, crewman, open your eyes!" And the frivolity begins. Stella's thought of everything.

The walls are bulkheads with glowing panels and consoles. Life-sized cutouts of the Voyager cast stand around the room. Tuvok at one of the punch bowls. Colored lights must be strung out underneath the wall hangings to mimic the effect of the control consoles being actually activated.

The big teleconferencing screen runs a Voyager episode. Novelists and grad students make a point of letting her know which props they brought from home. Some grin over to the pile of gifts, on a corner table. The pile seems large for a normal office going away party. Christina tries ignoring it.

Everyone wears a comm badge, the gold stylized triangle shape with a horizontal bar across its center. Someone asks, "Are these embroidered?"

"I'll have you know, crewman, that that comm badge is micro-milled duranium. You're looking at plasma-bonded gold and silver alloys. Circa twenty-three seventy-one."

"This is way better than that soap opera party," Daniel whispers to Marc.

And one of the gifts is in a small box, "Oh yeah. You gotta open that one."

"Do that one first."

"No, mine."

Christina jokes, reaches for a different one from the stack, "Not this one?"

"Tina!" Daniel, emboldened, actually places the smaller one, wrapped in the star-patterned paper, into her hands. Everyone's now nodding, "Open it." "G'wan." "She'll love it." "Oh, yeah."

Lieutenant pips; one black, and one gold. Daniel takes them from her and pins them on her shirt while Jean and Denise begin the first of many rounds of clapping which continues till the last goodbye gift is unwrapped and appreciated.

Christina nibbles on the party foods, loath to cut into the cake: her face airbrushed into a red and black Voyager uniform, two pips at the grey collar.

"…This baby contains a Universal Translator circuit, equipped with the linguistic analysis routines for basic translations, plus your critical conversational libraries of over two-hundred and fifty-three galactic civilizations." Marc even has his iPod with him, set to randomly play the comm signal's trilling beep. He tries to catch it every time by tapping on his chest, "Findley here."

"…Well, yeah, if you're talking the Rebel Alliance Duty Uniform, then yeah, you've got the traditional ST badge design over a golden triangle. But this is…"

"Nice comm badge, there crewman." Becomes a risqué comment. "Lovely pips, I might add." A saucy retort. Giggles, like a sleepover at two in the morning, everyone's loopy with the fun. God. She was gonna miss these guys like all mad crazy.

Daniel sits at the conference table with Christina and they spend a bit watching the Voyager episode on the big screen. "So did you decide yet what type of shipper you are?"

To end the goodbye bash, Stella slips out of the star-covered room and they hear her over Rose's intercom: her best computer voice, "Warning. Oxygen depletion of holodeck simulation for Office Farewell Party in 25 seconds. All crewmen report to your individual escape pods now. This is not a drill… Warning. Oxygen depletion of holodeck simulation for Office Farewell Party in 20 seconds. All crewmen…"

Christina stays to help with the clean-up. She sweeps napkins and forks and empty soda cups into the trash. Shoos Rose and Denise and a new girl, Jan, away from lifting the big black garbage bags, says, "Just open the back door and lift the dumpster lid. I got this. G'on. You've got families to get home to. We've got this covered."

Big hugs and last words on missing her. Her hard work. Her humor. Her laughter. Her face. "Okay," they joke, "maybe not your face…" Jan stands blushing, too new to know if she should join in with the ribbing. They all wave one last time and hold their purses and jackets, tap at their comm badges one last time in farewell. Office crew out.

A final wave from the glass entrance, and then it's only Stella and Christina left. The bags are all twist-tied and out at the dumpster, the tablecloths wiped down and refolded for the next time. "Thanks for all this—it was great."

"Think I might keep the lights up," Stella surveys the decorated walls of Conference Room B, the last thing that needs removal. "I like the look."

"Start wearing pips?"

"I could do worse." She lays a hand on Christina's shoulder, as they move to the door, "Got to tell you, dear. You'll be missed."

Christina doesn't hunch. Leans in, just a tad, "Oh, I think there'll be other Payroll folks you'll be able to lure in here."

And Stella surprises her by pulling her in closer for a motherly hug. Squeezes. "I meant Harrison."

It's Willis who takes her for the driving test. Then stands in line with her to get her license. She'd biked to Word of Mouth where they'd taken Willis' Ford Escort since that's what they practiced in. Harrison coming with her was out of the question. She'd rather die. And when she says so, Harrison beams. "Yeah." He concedes, "Don't need your old dad there for something like this."

He knows what's going unsaid. How if he were with her that would ruin the growing up and making him proud bit that's wrapped up in a such a big stage as this. So does Christina, especially the bit about bringing home the license and making him proud.

Well, she has the damn thing. Hates the photo. Doesn't recognize the girl there at all. Her weight's down into the 130's now and her face is still unfamiliar to her own eyes. Though Willis takes a peek and says, "Look just like your mom." After the license they go back to Word of Mouth and dish up a hunk of sookie, the cast iron skillet full of chocolate chip cookie, topped with soft vanilla ice cream. It dawns on her that Willis knew her mom before Harrison did.

They say they're celebrating that she passed with a healthy score, a whole 15 points away from the failure line. And they promise as they sit and eat that she'll take some sookie back to Harrison, too. In just a bit. Right after Christina's nerves settle.

Christina pushes the spoon down into the melted ice cream and asks about that novel Willis told her about. Wants to know, "What's it going to be about?" Really wants to know. She badgers him till he spills it.

Willis laughs, wipes his hands on the apron at his waist. "—bout a guy who runs a BBQ shop, gives it over to his son-in-law and spends the rest of the days sleuthing, getting himself into all kinds of trouble." The phone rings and he glances at it. Tonette. He laughs, "What else?"

She's so glad that they talk like this. Where would she be without Willis and the smell of smoked links and ribs?

Willis is off the phone and talk segues into the Sunday dinners they used to have back in Georgia where he was from. About the time he got down on his knees to propose to his then girlfriend, now wife of 42 years. How his Gram hit him with a damp dish towel for not warning her. "She woulda made some sookie if she'd 'a known it was a special occasion."

Willis' eyes shine at the memories. Christina's too, at the thought of such a life—full of family like that. What would she give to remember days like that?

What she wouldn't give. Willis waves away her ten-dollar bill, "This one's on the house, dear. Your money's no good here today. Time to get back on the road and go show your dad this new trophy of yours. So go saddle up that pretty bike and be sure to say hi from me. Tell him we need to see him around here more often. We got some smokin' wings with his name on 'em."

Christina smiles, promises Willis she won't forget, and sure enough when she gets home Willis' message is the first thing out of her mouth. Harrison says, "Yeah, I should get on over there. How's the old guy doing anyway?" When she coughs up the new license he wants to all but frame the damned thing. Beams. Says, "Wait. I'm getting the camera."

Chapter Eleven

THE BIG MOMENT. It's done. The fully refurbished and road-worthy original 1979 Westfalia waits in the driveway. They spent the night before loading the camper. And all during that charade Christina couldn't bring herself to speak up and tell him the truth.

"No, c'mer. Stand here." Harrison slaps at the fingers headed for Christina's mouth. "Stop that."

A step back and he checks his little flip-up viewfinder on his ancient Argoflex Seventy-Five 35mm. A box camera. He's positioning her next to The Van. It's a brilliantly sunny day, so there's no need for the camera's bulky flash gun.

With a step up, a step back, a loosening of his shoulders, Christina sighs. But Harrison is still fiddling. More head dips to the view finder and realignments, baby steps to the left then right back to his first position. Finally, he calls, "Hold it." And takes the first shot.

He moves her to the opened side door, where he can get

a picture with the pristine interior behind her. *Snap*. Walks her around to the front. Snap. "Just hold it a second while I—hold it. Now look at me, smile Chrissie."

She tries her best to look at the camera while Harrison tries his best to focus the thing and not get his own shadow in the shots. *Snap*. "One more, sweetie, look up at the rag top."

"Harrison." But he's busy adjusting the tripod now.

"We'll do the last one timed, with you and me in a shot." He turns her to the left, and runs back to check the framing, wanting both their heads in there. Sets the timer and hustles back to put his arm around her shoulder.

They both look up, at the wonder of green and cream striped canvas. Travel. The Open Road. 900 miles were just a start for her. Harrison says, "I know it in my bones. America awaits." He squeezes her to him one last time.

"Say, *adios*."

Snap.

So now, no more pictures to take. She has no other reason to go back in the house. To crawl into her own bed, shut her door and cry. Now all she has left to do is fess up or drive away.

Christina steps up into the driver's seat and rolls down the driver's window. Sitting and staring out of the shiny windshield, she sets her hands on the steering wheel. *Can I do this? Yeah. I can.*

Harrison's handed over the keys and he slides the side

door shut for her. It's a nice, solid noise. He raps twice on the door under her elbow. Still she keeps quiet. Harrison's face says it's because she's really going. "Well, baby—" then he waits for her to turn the ignition. "Use all your mirrors, right?"

"Right." She nods, and begins reciting. "Turn signals, yellow means slow down and nothing else. Change lanes responsibly. Easy at intersections."

"You forgot, 'Have fun'." He grins, stepping back. But those eyes. Those eyes.

He holds his shoulders squared, solid. Waves goodbye. And she rolls out into the street. Both their eyes wide with her sheer feat of combustible motion. Eyes wet with the loss this great gain has wrought.

As she shifts out of reverse, she hears the phone from inside and she waves him off. "Go get it! It might be the lady at the gallery." For a moment she worries it might be Danny. But she tells herself, *nah*.

And she heads on down the street, gripping the steering wheel and checking all her mirrors. *Fucking blind spots*. And strangely, she forgets for a block or two that she's only going across town.

Forty blocks later she sets the Van in park behind the apartment and makes her way upstairs.

Christina has no reason to be in motion now. No one to cook for, wash up after. No loads of work clothes in the laundry, no need to pick up skirts and jackets from the dry cleaners. No office to sit in or cat to tend. She can be wide awake, up for a full eighteen hours of the day's twenty-four, or she can sleep through the same period of time. And often does. No cat's paw at dawn, no gentle tapping, *Lady? Lady? Hey, Lady, feed me!*

Only her laptop and Voyager were constants. She doesn't even make up a change of address card for the mail at Harrison's house. Days pass and she never rolls her bike in from the patio. After nightfall she finds her way around the space in the dark. Trips over the sleeping bag on the floor, but knows the bathroom door is nine more paces ahead.

She hears herself say out loud, "I'll get lamps soon." but never seems to get up to the point of doing it.

Dawn finds Christina eating a handful of blueberries from the fridge. Her big meals are tuna sandwiches on toasted rye, chopped celery and golden raisins, mixed in with the curry powder and extra dark mustard. Apple sliced in wedges on the side. Or she drags herself upright and goes for a chicken and rice burrito from Gardino's on the corner at Ritter Road.

She never manages to finish off a full meal in a go, but tosses the near half of the burrito into trash, instead of putting it in the fridge where it'll go hard as rock while she ignores it's there. Doesn't think to sit on the orange plastic seats in front of the take-out window and get some fresh air, watch the traffic.

The place stays empty for nearly three weeks.

But there in a shop downstairs, on the way back from getting a burrito, she sees a mission-style recliner. Mostly wide slats of oak. But for the seat and backrest, she thinks it's needlepoint. The living room is too narrow for a full-sized sofa, but this would fit. In a way it reminds her of Harrison. And Jeffrey helped her get it upstairs. So kind. He doesn't ask when she might be getting curtains for the place.

Then one day she's just fed up with Harrison's T-shirts nearly falling off her shoulder. Her shorts are hanging so much lower on her frame. She goes out to The Van and finds the minuscule sewing kit Harrison cached there for her trip. Finds the tape measure and brings it upstairs, too.

She can't believe it. First the apartment and now this. Can it be true? The tape measure isn't lying, Christina's rechecked all the inches three times. Wrote the numbers down new every time. Exhales and pooches her stomach out a bit, to make certain the numbers for her waist are a true measure, yep; she writes it down on her pad for the last time. Waist: 28 inches. Bust: 36. Hips: 38. *God. I can buy size tens.*

She looks through all the catalogs Harrison loaded for 'light reading'; that she's now stacked for recycling. Title 9, Uncommon Goods, *where the fuck is it?* TravelSmith, Sundance, ah, at last: The Territory Ahead. *Here we go, baby.*

Christina has to get up and go find a pen to write with, the mechanical pencil she's tried using keeps snapping its lead as she grips too tightly, presses too hard. First comes the big X's on the items that strike her. Tops mostly, things that won't look too girly. That hang loose.

Scanning for the pieces that won't look too unnatural on the old body she mistakenly still sees in her own mind, (in spite of the tape measure and the facts on her list). She takes a real deep breath, then starts at page one again, crossing out most of her first choices.

Remembering back to how beautiful her mother always looked, she crosses out the two jackets that remind her of what *classy feminine women* wear. She sticks to cotton tops, to the Henleys and the denims and chinos. Camisoles are out of the question. In the end she only keeps pullovers, jettisons the cardigans and things with angora or tapestry in the descriptions. Skips *The Velvet Collection* entirely. Why can't she just find stuff that looks good with an open necktie and a panama hat?

In the end; she's written with such pressure, anyone knowing Braille might guess at the items on her pad of paper. But she does have a list, now. *I can do this.* She logs on and keys in the URL from the back page. Body shaking. A long intake of breath. Wipes her hands on her jeans and repositions the pad. Pushes up her sleeves.

But she can't. Has to stand and move away. Punches at her own thigh and starts walking around the room in long lunging steps, Cossack style, from the pad on the floor to the recliner and back to the laptop again.

Balance. More. Yes. Keep. Going.

Each step a command. Till her thighs are burning and her calves cramp. "FUCK!" she screams.

Then with her throat raw and a bit out of breath from the strides, she sits down, rubs her jaw and notices her teeth are clenched. She shakes her hands like a limbering pianist, bends over the keyboard, "Okay." She decides this is one thing she can't let herself run away from. And she begins with the New Customer Registration form on the login page.

She writes real letters to ARCoBAL from the board. Asks if she'd mind re-mailing the enclosed so it went to Harrison from there. Christina sends the postage and a thanks to Char for helping in this subterfuge thing. It's all planned out, forum folk from up and down the California coast all get letters with instructions of when to mail them off. If it didn't fail, it might look like she's really traveling.

The letter she writes him says dumb stuff of no consequence. Promising to send on non-existent photos as soon as she figures out where she stored the cable for the camera to her laptop. Saying Char had a dog and cat. Lies. Fibs that make Christina miss Nicky. She feels—vacant— writing all that deception.

With the apartment, now that the clothes start arriving from the mail ordering spree, it's easy. She's let herself go. Not sure what it was that finally broke, but something had. Maybe it's because Char's forwarded her a letter from Harrison. Things are looking good. He's falling for the ruse. Really believes she's taking her time and exploring the beaches and camp sites from San Diego up to Ventura. Leg One of her journey.

Christina finds an oak table with carved legs at the same shop downstairs. Three feet by three. A solid piece, it looks to be at least 70 years old. Inlaid quarter-sawn planks for the lift-off tabletop. The lady in the shop, dark curly hair, a nice smile, high cheekbones, lays a veined hand on the wood, caresses the grain, "If you use it with the leaf extended you've got another two feet on the length." Explains it's a hide-away type of a drop leaf style. "More to it, but the hidden kind."

For another week Christina thinks over owning it, before she acts. Clothes were one thing. But this… she's that uncomfortable about having *stuff*.

But just in time, she goes back downstairs, says she'll buy it. She figures she'll use the table for a work space in the little empty bedroom. Maybe find out what software it takes to make videos like on her J/7 searches on YouTube and download it onto her laptop. If she ever gets that brave.

Suzanne, the shop owner, seems glad to see her again, saying, "Didn't think you were gonna be back for this. I nearly sold it yesterday, the guy said he'd bring his wife in for a look on Tuesday." She takes an extra $25 off the ticketed price. "Lucky you; sniped him." Tells Christina, with a wink, "Now you can buy a lamp or a clock next time you're in." Runs her hand over the piece again as she walks past it to the door with Christina, "I'll call Jeffrey," Suzanne promises.

Klingon#1: It's final, kitty cat had to be put down.

TulipAna: {{{Klingon#1 !!}}}

The following week it's a parsons table for in front of the living room window. Things are coming together. She uses the van for the larger pieces she finds from surfing Craigslist postings. Who knew all this was out there? Sure, she's driving out of town up as far as Palm Desert and Coachella, but Christina wonders if her mother was ever this happy, building a nest on her own for the very first time.

There are over 700 members in the Ready Room, and a healthy percentage of them are there to write Trek fan fiction or are posting the YouTube videos they've created. Discussing just how they go about making these little gems. They're Christina's only friends, now that she's in hiding. No Harrison, Willis, Stella or Jean to talk to anymore.

During the afternoons, she reads the pages of posts with folks chatting about editing techniques and scene selections. Which software grabs scenes, which converts IFO & VOB files. Fonts for credits and when the fast cut works best for songs with a heavy beat.

Wishes hit, that she had some phone numbers, just to be able to express herself out loud. Hear her own voice once in a while. She asks so many questions: What it takes to use the songs you've got on your iPod. How to deal with region 1 and region 2 DVDs. Song matches, fade ups. This could be college, if there were degrees in Voyager Vids.

She refrains from buying any Star Trek Voyager home décor she stumbles across. It's not an easy call. Concentrates on outfitting the kitchen instead: the basics like a cheese grater and a collapsible colander. A rice steamer and one plate, a bowl and mug from a thrift store. Unrolls her knife kit and sets them lovingly in a folded towel, touches each blade. Then shuts the drawer on Harrison's ghost.

The living room now looks like it could be a canvas. She sticks to the Mission motif. What Suzanne at her shop calls 'Craftsman bungalow' style. Finding a set of matching lamps at Suzanne's is a new high; those amber mica shades and wrought iron bases. At night they glow golden; when Christina bothers to light them.

In the dark of her living room, while watching Voyager on her laptop, Christina notices the emptiness. How she misses Harrison and Nicky something fierce, like the feeling is a spoon's scoop of reality, out of her airways; something vital now gone. But she doesn't miss having a TV set at all. Although it's also true that her shoulders are sore from all the time she spends online.

And so, of course, Suzanne notices her posture and asks. And hearing the problem, mentions, "Maybe you need end tables to go under the lamps."

It's become a beautiful place. Nearly all in order, friends on the board. Maybe the bedroom will get done next. At least now, when Christina remembers the lamps, she's not in the dark. One Saturday, she takes the plunge and asks Nomad, if she'll be willing to forward letters too.

It's then she finds out Nomad lives in El Centro, too.

Except for her sleeping pattern, which refuses to act right and be realigned, and the physical loneliness, Christina thinks she'll be okay, finding out this latest news.

THE THINKER Thread:

****

ITV: What's the one thing you've always wanted to know?

LARGEMARGE: How to calculate star dates.

LARGEMARGE: What's the one thing you *never* wanted to know?

ITV: How a cat's purr box works.

Nov_Kid: What do you like best about this board?

LemonSkye: We don't discuss minute plot points as if they really mattered. We discuss them because they *do* really matter.

Christina dreams that Harrison is on a pier, and his hair is on fire. Except it's not Harrison. It's an alien from Voyager. And he's not on fire. He's getting transported. But he's failed the maneuver; he's stuck; not going, not staying. Which is why his hair seems alight.

When she wakes up she can't breathe right. Can practically smell that ionized air of the fiery aborted transport. Tells herself, "I've got to get out more."

****

TulipAna: I think NOW has arrived.

ARCoBAL: *GRIN* Like Janeway says: Do It.

Christina's not been on the freeways. So, of course, she takes to the task with such one-minded diligence Harrison would be proud. First there's the figuring out total mileage. ARCoBAL's address, some city called Huntington Beach. What time they've agreed to meet in another town farther north called Seal Beach.

She subtracts the distance from the hotel she's found to the meeting spot and converts that to bike minutes since they plan 'a little jaunt', as Char put it. And she'll be riding up to the Seal Beach.

So there she is, 3 o'clock in the morning and sitting in the van, a cup of hot tea in her hands, warming up the engine for the full length of one whole song, before starting out, just like Harrison taught her to.

Chapter Twelve

WHILE PACKING FOR this trip, the thought comes to her that she'll be driving crosswise through the state to meet up with a person she feels she knows but has never seen before. Christina holds one of the new Henleys up to her shoulders, decides: *Take it.* She tosses it onto one of the stacks on her sleeping bag. *Did I portray myself* right *on the boards?* It circles her mind. Will Char take one look at *Christina* and think: what a fraud?

Maybe this is a horrible idea, part of her frets, then she scoops up the five things she's considered wearing for the trip and pulls them to her chest. She hates all these colors. And the clothes' hug is also tremendously unsatisfying. *Where's a cat to hug at moments like this?* In the end she remembers to pack her list and take her new camera to get some real shots to send back to Harrison. She needs a nap.

✷

Once the lights of the city are falling away behind in her rear-view mirrors, ahead seems to be an ocean of dark. Christina drives with the window down and she can smell the fields to her left and right. That acrid leaf and vine and soil aroma of field produce. It's at Dixie Drain #4 that she comes up to the desert and thinks of Harrison. The desert and his paintings, though he probably goes East, the other side of Date City, for those sunrises.

The freeway narrows to the single lane and she lets herself move into a state of driving and non-driving. Out loud it surprises her to hear her voice: "I was born to this." Did Harrison know? Was *that* the reason for all the pushing? *God.* She feels like she could drive through the night for the rest of her life. *I'm really on the road. Damn.*

To while away the time, she practices: "Oh, please," No. too weird. "Really just—" Yuck. "Hi, I'm Tina but you can—" Nah. Pounds on the steering wheel. She switches songs on the iPod, squinting into the oncoming headlights on the Interstate. *Shit…*

"Call me Ana," the dogged voice begs out loud again.

Somewhere on the night's drive she promises herself, *If I make it through this, I'll really take a second shot at that pesky Item #7.* Learn Stuff.

Sunrise catches Christina from behind, about an hour from San Diego. It beams into every one of her rear-view mirrors, right in the retina. She curses having forgotten sunglasses. Promises herself all future trips will start at midnight and she'll be off the road by sun up. She's practicing success in her head; seeing future trips already.

The road passes under the van with her humming along to the music she had played all night. She blesses the guys who came up with the method of playing shuffled songs on a continuous loop. The only way to drive. Most of the night's been passed with a new idea for a J/7 video with every song that she hears. Way better than cruise control.

At a motel in Huntington Beach she asks the girl at the front desk about her planned bike routes up into Seal Beach, and the clerk nods yes, "You can get there on the bike trail, it's mostly flat. About nine plus miles, I think. Or I can call an Uber, it'll get you there too, but way, way quicker."

"Do you have a map? I really want to bike. I'm just looking at how to hook up with an actual road instead of PCH? Is that doable?"

She recognizes Char right off the bat, even without the purple shirt. Christina pats her hair and worries she looks crappy after the 200 plus mile drive, then the beach trail. *Why didn't I leave yesterday afternoon? Get a good night's sleep and a longer shower before showing up?* Well. Too late now.

Aside from her height Char's just like she said she'd be. Round and happy. But nowhere near the short and chubby person she's always alluded to being on the boards. Here's that smile from the picture she posted in the TIME FOR YOUR CLOSE-UP thread.

"I wasn't sure it was you. Till I saw the bike helmet." Char holds out her hand, but Christina reaches past that and freaks her own self out by giving Char a quick hug hello. Not her style at all. She pulls away, blushes, looking for a place to sit in the tiny café.

Char, ignoring the red face, just asks, "Wanna order? They've got some killer omelets here. Seal Beach's finest. Folks bike down on weekends along the bike trail that runs along the six-oh-five freeway, on the San Gabriel. You can pick it up in Rosemead, even as far up as Duarte. You know those areas?"

Christina waits a second, makes sure there's no more words tumbling out before answering. "No, sorry, I don't." Forehead creased, biting her lip.

"That's okay. It's not gonna be on the quiz."

She can't stop smiling, touching her napkin and fork. Christina wants to banter back but the words don't come. "Ah, no. Just from maps. They're on the list though." *Should I call her by her board name? Or something a bit more formal? How should I bring that up? Do I smell from the ride? Is my hair okay?*

A waitress slaps two menus on the table, "Be right with you gals. Read up." So Christina busies her hands with the list of omelets and muffin choices, and the selection of fruit juices. Char is the first one to say something after the waitress takes their orders and their coffee cups are filled.

"I was scared shitless meeting you. Thought up all kinds of pithy lines on the way over." Her eyes crinkle, she pats her jeans pocket, "Wrote a few of them down."

Christina exhales, risks scratching at her itchy temples, tries to keep her hands from touching the top of her head, "I was hoping I wouldn't smell so rank."

Both of them grin now—Char laughs, "Best laid plans, huh?"

"We can do anything you'd like. I've got the day free."

"Well. It's kind of geeky," Christina starts.

"Legoland, right? I thought you looked the type."

"Nah. Even worse—" Christina's blush resurfaces along her neck, "Can we go see the CSULB Campus? Walk around and I dunno, maybe go to their bookstore?"

"Ooo, you madcap kid."

"Is that a yes?"

"Sure, we can do that. I went there. Did we say that in the posts? Oh you'll love it, it's a great school. I'll go back and finish some year."

"Why aren't you still going?"

Char likes looking at the waves they can see from their table, "A convergence of reasons. A perfect storm of *Whoa*."

"Mysterious."

"Nah. Just bad timing. I'll tell you the whole story someday. Let's just say it's one rich in the Big D's. Deception, Death, Depression & Damn! Then She Did What?"

"God." It's the only thing Christina can think to say, and she surprises herself hearing it, "Must have hurt."

"Yeah. Well, you know, things come up. Life's what happens while we're busy making plans."

"Yeah."

"So I had to stop going. First things first. Maybe I'll go back to it. I'm not dead yet." Char straightens from leaning on the table, "I could look at the ocean all day, but time's a-wasting." She taps Christina's helmet, "What type of work do you do? When you're not on the road visiting?"

"Office work. When I can get it."

The campus is enormous, and so green in every direction that Christina's arms rise goosebumps seeing it all. Jacaranda trees are in bloom. Lavender for days. "Peterson Hall." Char points as they walk. "Brotman Hall." The whole of the place seems to be situated on steep inclines and down-hills, or flat expanses that seem to go on forever.

Char, pointing left and right as they cross the acre-wide quad, near the library steps, has Christina not knowing which way to turn and look first. "I was here for five semesters. But I didn't live on campus. I had a place up in Duarte, that's like, thirty, thirty-two miles north of here. All one freeway though."

Thirty-two miles to come to school every day. Christina can't even imagine what that must be like. Char flicks her wrist again, pointing out a tall building as they walk back across that huge lawn, "Macintosh. Humanities."

Upper Campus, Lower Campus. The Chart Room. East Campus. The Nugget Pub and Grill. It's a city all on its own. They stop in the Forty-Niner University bookstore and Christina's breath just leaves her. She wobbles, grabs Char's arm. "Holy shit."

This is surely a dream; Christina spies a university catalog, searches its cover, asks, "Can anyone buy one of these?"

She just can't stop smiling as Char points her down the aisle for Biology and it's there that Christina finds the California Coastal Access Guide. Revised and Expanded, Sixth Edition. She opens it at random, and sees descriptions of campgrounds, trails. Harrison would shit. Recreation areas, bike paths. Maps and location addresses. Flipping a page, she reads: The Southern Sea Otter…

They had her at the *campgrounds*.

In the library they take the stairs up to the third floor to walk around the stacks. Christina's hand trails along the rows and rows of books. *#7 on my list could be the only one I touch if I came here. If I let myself stay.*

"Will you do something with me? Not for reals, but, like as a help? Like, I dunno, role playing?" They've sat at one of the wide study tables, to get off their feet and decide where to go eat for dinner tonight.

"Will it involve safe words?" Char rears back from the table, to take a quick look around. "This is a pretty open space we're in here."

"Please?" Christina's grip on her Coastal Access Guide

tightens. "I don't think I can do it alone."

Char studies her face. So serious. "Sure. What'd you have in mind?"

Christina's shoulders relax and they drop an inch to two. From out of her backpack she pulls the catalogs from the bookstore. Setting out one for her, one for Char. And turns them each to the registration forms. Follows that with the list of the Schedule of Classes, two pens. Like a sacred ritual.

Christina wiggles in her chair. Takes a deep breath, folds her hands up under her armpits, elbows tight at her sides. Shoulders hunched for a blow. But then comes an exhale, two of them. She nods and pulls one hand free to tap at her catalog, in an undertone saying, "Talk to me like I'm seven. Use small words. What do you do here? How is this done?"

So Char explains the concept of the GE core, General Education credits, how you need so many classes from Column A so many from Column B, on down the list. "It's what's meant by a liberal education. The major is something different entirely." She's careful, makes sure to point as she reads the GE subjects off: "See? Social Sciences, Humanities. Hard Sciences; Physical and Biological, Mathematics. Writing. Foreign Languages." Patient as hell with all of the questions spilling out of Christina.

"You have to learn a language?"

"Yep. Required." Tap, tap.

"Klingon count?"

Char flips through some of the pages, checking to be sure, "Sadly, no. Imagine auditing that one."

"…but the ones numbered 100 and 200, they don't have to be the only choices, right? For any of the columns? I can do this—" *tap, tap.* Christina leans in close and reads out, "ENGL 180? Appreciation of Literature?" Flips some more pages and grins, checking to make sure it wasn't a mistake, that it really was true, "Or this one, BIOL 158 – MARINE BIOLOGY and the California Coast?"

"Yep. You got it. The basic 100 & 101 classes are for those guys who just want to clear the credits."

"Take a class without learning? Are you serious?"

Char just stares. Is probably thinking, *What a newbie…* So Christina keeps reading and asking.

"Then you get to do what you want, the major stuff you explained, like Software Designing? After all this is done?"

"Unless you have to drop, like I did." *Ah.* A light goes off. Char's voice nearly breaks.

Christina asks, "So where does that safe word come in?"

"Now comes the hard part." Christina exhales and apologizes, then explains practicing success in her head. How she wants the two of them to do this little exercise like it's for real. Like it's truly going to happen in her life. Her. At a University. A place like this school.

So each one fills out the courses they'd like to take for the upcoming fall session. Christina's Coastal Access Guide is forgotten at her elbow for the moment. Char glances over at the other form, busy under Christina's quick jotting. She'll admit later that she's never seen such tiny, restricted handwriting.

Christina holds her schedule out at arm's length. Makes a face but nods, her tongue peeking between her teeth. She leans back into the chair, and blows out a long breath, like hearing her dentist tell her, *looks like we won't have to drill after all.*

"Think you're really gonna enroll now?" Char asks.

The question makes Christina jump. She grabs Char's list and her own, the two catalogs as well. Sweeps everything into her backpack. The pens follow. A disappearing act like none Char's seen before. "Hell no!"

Char just laughs, then risks reaching over and rubbing Christina's head, bumps her with her shoulder, "Too weird."

"This was a great time, Char. Thanks so much."

"*De nada.* I had a lot of fun." She holds her side, grimaces, "But boy, Tina, you gotta remember to slow down when you bike." Their voices trail off, shy now. No banter in reserve. An awkward try at another hug, this one failing miserably over their handlebars.

"So next time I can come out and you can show me El Centro, right?"

Christina laughs at the thought, "I'd invite you but then you'd have to kill yourself."

"That bad, huh?"

"You'd have more fun stranded in the Delta Quadrant for seven fracking years."

Luckily Christina can go back to the hotel room and sleep for the next several hours. She steers back south, down PCH, and at the hotel locks the bike in The Van before heading up to her room for a good long nap. She sleeps till midnight.

There's nothing to get back home for. But still, she's flying on the drive back to El Centro. Her mind is alight with imagining herself at that campus. Talking to real people. Making friends. Sitting in classes and always asking questions. Every book in that bookstore at her fingertips. Maybe even an apartment on the beach. Seal Beach. *God what a wonderful name. Seal Beach.*

The mountains around her and the new book on the passenger's seat, along with a decorated box for papers or photos that caught her eye back in Huntington Beach, lead her to consider talking to Harrison. Calling him up and saying she'll be coming back to town. Saying "Come with me for those 900 miles before I settle down to school. What do you think?"

She fantasizes Harrison agreeing, "We can get Nicky a collar and leash. I can see what a great driver you are."

And her answering, "Safety's my motto. We can meet up with all my board friends, all along the route."

Wouldn't he get a kick out of that? The things they could do this one last time. Harrison would have so much fun. God. A real trip, *and* school, too. Talk about your dreams falling right into your lap. How many times can that happen in one life?

Once Christina is back, she leaves everything but the new book in The Van and heads upstairs for another nap. She doesn't wake up for a full eleven hours.

Christina looks around. Awake with a jerk now, but not refreshed. *It must be nightfall.*

Boy, she feels tired. Her eyes fall on the Costal Access book and the trip comes back to her. She lifts her head from the pillow, then decides to take a shower. In the kitchen she eats a handful of week-old grapes and wonders about getting her butt in gear and unpacking from the trip. *Nah.* She doesn't even feel like logging in. In the growing dimness, all she can try is lying back down. Her hand on all that knowledge; she yawns. *One more hunk of shut-eye,* she promises herself. *I'm bushed.*

The next time she's come awake she feels pretty sure she can keep upright. Pretty sure. Not certain. Can't figure out what's in the air that makes it so hard to be in the here and now. *Felt so vibrant on the coast.*

After pulling herself around the room in a fog, she considers where to keep her new book, finally stashing it in her bedroom closet. In the bottom of a laundry basket full of old summer clothes from last year that don't fit anymore. Now that she's certain she seems fully awake, things feel *wrong* somehow. Christina doesn't know why; just feels funny now that she's made it back to El Centro. Having the book sitting out in the open might have been the problem.

She realizes that's too silly to allow it to be a thing, so she talks herself into getting on with the unpacking. Remembering. *Shit, I'll have to go back down to The Van.*

But when she does, it's then she realizes she's left her laptop behind somewhere. *At the hotel? Ah shit.* In her mind's eye she sees it there; in the bathroom. On the toilet tank. *Damn it. What was I thinking?*

It's a phone call to the front desk to find out—yes. They have it. "Didn't the manager give you a call?—Oh. Well. So sorry. He said he would." The voice on the phone doesn't know what went wrong. Apologizes. And, "Yes, we can overnight it this morning. No worries." Christina hangs up. Relieved. *What's a day or two without contact, tired as I feel?*

Chapter Thirteen

HE DAYS OF Heil Street with Nicky, the pair sprawling on the sofa watching TV with a big gulp and some chips, are so far behind her she feels like she's been transported to a new world.

The only thing about no laptop is she feels there are no other sentient beings to reach out to. And while in real life she handles this, for some reason without the J/7 boards she feels like her family is gone. She spends the night in her recliner after dinner, reading about the California Coast.

The pages and pages of knowing here in this one book dazzle her. Marine life, natural reserves and refuges, and geology. Historic names of the California tribes: Chumash, the Miwok and the Tolowa; at one time 300 thousand in population and 100 plus dialects of over twenty languages up and down the 1,100 miles of shoreline. And that's just in the Introduction Chapter.

She reads the textbook like it's a novel and fights it, but

finally, slips a bookmark in between the pages when her hands and eyes grow too tired to keep learning.

She doesn't even head for her sleeping bag. Instead, she just pulls her maroon throw over her shoulders and sets the recliner to somewhat flat, waking up feeling like she's slept for a week on a bed of lavender and warm feathers. Dreaming of the acres of stuff to learn.

The laptop arrives in good order and the first thing she does is sweep all the packing aside and plug everything in. Then she logs in and checks the board. It feels like she's been away for centuries, and she moves from thread to thread, not skipping any of the topics, so glad to be back home.

Two days pass and Christina's not sure what went wrong, but Char won't answer any of her DMs. Christina's even tried Skype, and nothing. She has no idea what she might have said or done, and no phone to ask. No way of finding out.

Had she failed to do something once she got back from the trip? Or that last try at a hug that melted away to nothing? She breaks down and sends a personal message to FaeLight07, asking for guidance, and if she can, a meeting over coffee.

TulipAna: Have you been talking to Char lately?

FaeLight07: Why yes, child I have *wink* *wink* you should be ashamed.

TulipAna: What??? What's she said?

FaeLight07: Ooo la la.

TulipAna: ????

FaeLight07: heard it was quite a time. I believe Hospitalization was mentioned. I can't sleep at night with the images THAT conjured of your time together. She says she may write a Fan Fic piece or two, incorporating or should I say, commemorating some of those positions—oh to be young again.

TulipAna: ?!?! total and unmitigated lies. What's going on here?

FaeLight07: as I heard it you were quite the dog, you. *wink* *wink* *nudge* *nudge*

TulipAna: Well you heard wrong. Bye now.

She doesn't just log off—she shuts down the laptop. Appalled. That wasn't the way it was. How could Char say that? She pushes the laptop away from her on the table. Stunned.

God. *What else have they been saying back and forth about me?* She reaches, pulls at the USB cable and stands. Stays off the boards after that. Her face flames every time Fae's words swim up to taunt her: *Ooo la la.*

Christina sets her incoming email from anyone on the board to go directly to trash. Empties it without once looking to see who's written. First the DMs that come her way are ignored. Then she uninstalls Skype. Shaken to her core.

Has no idea that Char's sister is forwarding mail because Char's in the hospital with appendicitis. That Fae was only pulling her leg, teasing her with replies like they all post from time to time.

Like family do on occasion.

The first letter. It comes from Arcadia, no note along with it, just the forwarded letter from Harrison. His scrawny penmanship: the C/O line reading Ms. Char Paris. (thank you) and a happy face next to it. It reminds Christina to get the pictures developed and mailed off to him. But can she? Now? Who else can she get to do that for her? After all she's done to hide from the forum members.

Harrison's letter, written a day before she set out for her trip, is full of good cheer and happy times with Nicky. Sitting on the couch and watching porn on cable together. 'High times for bachelors', he writes, 'but don't worry, Nicky's not getting high. And neither is your old man.'

But she can see it's not all that. His writing runs downward off each of the blue lines on the paper. She turns the page over and reads: 'Here's the roots part of things. Now that you have the wings…' and her heart squeezes.

Contact at last. After the loss of the board Christina's been so bereft.

'Just a wee trip down memory lane here, now that you're too far away to hit me for bringing stuff like this up. (hah-ha-ha) Remember me paying you a dollar every time you took a shower without being reminded to? You were what, eleven, twelve? Viv thought you should be more of a lady, get into grooming and hair sprays and what shoes matched what belt and stuff.'

Christina doesn't want to be reminded of her dorky

years. Wishes Harrison is a bit less lonely. A bit more willing to focus on his todays instead of these yesterdays. But still. She's not been gone that long. Maybe this is a phase all dads have to go through. Once they decide about the real trip up the coast, there'd be plenty of time for reminiscing. She pulls a diet soda from the fridge. Grabs a few cashews from a jar and sits back down, sliding her feet into her sleeping bag. The hiss of the opened can and the rustle of the page and she gets back to reading:

'Dumb. You've always been who you were gonna be. And the 'you' you were has always been fine with me. Wish we all knew enough about ourselves as early as you seemed to. You make me proud. I miss you.'

She runs her fingers on his sign-off line,

Harrison

Maybe she should go home. Stop all this stupidness.

The days are long. And without the board she sleeps nearly every one of them all away. By the end of the week, when Christina showers and then steps on the scale, she finds she's dropped another four pounds since the beach.

No appetite. No board. No reason to be awake. She ignores the recliner and goes back to the sleeping bag Stops turning on lamps when she does wake to find the dark has come again.

One morning comes and she realizes she needs some food. At the bottom of the stairs she tells herself, *I'm going to drive over to Word of Mouth*. Get herself some BBQ and hugs from Willis.

But in The Van, she finds the map of the trip on the passenger seat. Stares at the green highlighter path out of the desert to the water. Remembers the laughing and the waves. All that open area of the campus.

In the driver's seat she sits and cries for a good ten minutes; can't get herself to stop. There in the parking spot behind her building, where no one can see she's home.

She wipes her eyes and climbs the stairs back to the sleeping bag.

Christina doesn't dream now. It's a sleep of the dead. Where there's no tribe. No group of people with eyes like hers at all. She hasn't checked her email in a week and a half, hasn't been on the boards either. No messaging with anyone. Especially not Char.

Jeffrey is the one to come up and hand her a small stack of letters and stuff, "The Mail carrier knows I'm the manger. Said your box was getting too full. And since I had your key for the trip you made… She wouldn't hand it over to just anybody. So don't worry." His eyes wander the room, worried. But nothing looks amiss. "She asked if I'd sign for the registered one. Consider me the building's receptionist."

Probably just junk mails, Christina thinks. Too weary to create any other scenario. She takes it all in a neat stack with a rubber band around it. "There were a few real pieces in there. I saw handwriting on the pink one." She looks down and nods. Thanks him, "Flu." She sniffs.

Not fooling anyone. While he watches she flips things

one by one into the rectangular wicker trash basket near the front door. Out. Out. Out. Then there's something real. In her hand is a letter, postmark from in town.

"Yep. A friend of mine." She taps it.

Christina pushes her hair off her forehead and smiles her best at Jeffrey. "Thanks. For coming up." Then she moves to close her door. Before looking at Char's letter, or tearing it up, she finds another one from Harrison, sent from Char again. Still no note.

Jeffery waves, a sweet smile, then Christina closes the door. His shadow passes her window as she pulls her legs up into the recliner to read Harrison's latest.

'Sold another painting. Stella's a real champion of the stuff. The Gallery Lady says she can maybe get me a showing. Nothing major. But still. Not the swap meet, you know? One of the pieces Stella even took on for her office. Says to tell you it's going in Conference Room B. That, 'You'd know'. How's that for moving in the right circles. I'm going corporate!'

She skips ahead, scans, trying to see what he's hiding. What's really going on. Maybe she should write to Stella. Get the real scoop.

'...that look on your face that Christmas you were seven and I talked your mom into letting me build you a chalkboard and desk so you could play school? Instead of some dumb doll house. Remember that? With that indented groove for your chalk and eraser? Just twenty little pieces of colored chalk, but you'd have thought I'd built the world for you...'

Love, (and hisses from Nicky)

Your dad.

She flips the page over. But there's no more. That's it. Things are way too normal with him and Christina doesn't like it.

It takes a while for her to read the letter from Char. Days pass without her thinking about it again, or the registered letter it implores her to open as soon as she gets it.

Christina lets the sun go down again without turning on a light. The darkness comes and she lets her eyes acclimate to the dimness. She sits. Numb. Minutes bled into hours and stillness is all that occurs. No tears. She feels too anesthetized for that.

She can see the words she's read from Stella's email. The one that has finally caught up with her now that she's bothered to look.

From: Stella Davis
To: Christina Paul
Sent: Thursday, May 12, 6:19:12 PM
Subject: Tina, PLEASE READ THIS.

Harrison took his life on the 9th.

I'm sorry you're on the road and not here for this news in person. No one wanted you to get these words in such a remote manner. I'm so sorry, dear. This isn't the way I know Harrison would have wanted it; if he was truly in a right state of mind… No one knows for sure but it looks like he planned all this out to make sure you weren't home when it happened.

Harrison came by the office with four new

canvases, a box he wanted me to forward you, and your cat Nicky, on a leash. Three days before they found his body he'd made plans with a mortuary, (I believe a Danny Blakely notified the police). Once we track you down and you're back in town I can see you get everything he left. Nicky made quite an impression at the office but now he/she's at my house. So don't worry on that front.

Willis didn't get a visit but he was sent a letter and Harrison specified an immediate cremation. Made it quite clear he didn't want you notified until all was settled.

Come home.

Stella

Christina could've been home with him. Could have stopped whatever it was that got to him. Protected him from those damned dreams of rising water. Been his life preserver.

She moves with a jolt. Stands and reaches for her helmet and bike key and is out the door.

The Walgreen doors slide open and the interior's brightness assaults her. *Everything should be black*, she thinks. *All of it.*

…Harrison took his life on the 9th.

Her head is down, and she only raises her chin to read the aisle signs overhead as she prowls the store. She knows her tears are obvious. She feels them, stiffened, on her face; no matter how many times she swipes at her eyes and nose.

No one and everyone at the same time seems to be staring, until Christina finds the scissors and hurries with them back home.

Chapter Fourteen

Darkness feels like some comfort. No one can see her streaming eyes.

Christina stands in her bathroom, bent at the waist, her nose clogged, and the breathing none too easy either, which she's given up on trying to control. Bent over like this, her thick wavy hair falls to nearly mid-thigh. So long that the furious pace of brush strokes from her nape don't reach all the way to the strand's tips.

The brush in her hand feels punishing, quick with each sweeping stroke, trying to wipe away something that she knows will be as permanent as the scar on her ankle. Soon, she has the whole wavy mess all in a palmful's grasp. Then *flip. Flip. Flip.* And the ponytail is captured in a scrunchy, a waterfall effect when she straightens up, reaching for the scissors.

✳

Struggling, hissing, "Goddamn it." with the cardboard and plastic of the scissor's packaging.

And Harrison's voice comes in on tiptoe, there in the little bathroom: 'Now if we only had a pair of… scissors…' and her sobbing breaks into laughter. Christina throws the imprisoned shears into her tub with so much force she had to skip to the side when they bounce right back out at her feet.

'Breathe baby.' Harrison voice nags. And that echoed authority causes a crashing wave to wash over her rocky state of *right now*. Like the shock of a simultaneous sneeze and fart at the dinner table, she can't stop laughing now.

Weary now, she bends for the scissors and wipes at her eyes. Deals with the stubborn packaging. And begins cutting through all those years.

Willis' letter, alluded to in Fae's pink envelope, tells Christina about the funeral. Fae, not sure about letting anyone know where Christina is. And Willis, only writing to say they want to find Christina. Not a word about Harrison. Just asking, 'Can you give this to her if she comes your way?'

Fae notes that none of the boards various emails were being answered, nor the DMs; 'So maybe all is being handled, and you're all caught up in whatever's going on back at home.' They hope to hear from her soon. They miss her. And all send virtual hugs; {{{{TuplipAna}}}}.

It can't be real. A perfect storm of no one talking to anyone else. Classic Fan Fiction fodder, Christina thinks, angst like this can't be manufactured any other way.

Stella's email and Willis' letter. These are the only bits of contact to let Christina know Harrison planned this all and there's nothing she can go back to now and try to fix.

'BabyGirl,' Willis wrote… *'Everything was done.'*

He wants her to come home just the same. She can stay at their place. Tonette says for as long as she needs.

'There were folks at the memorial from pretty far around. You would've been proud of that. A Mr. Vincent Moore came down from San Francisco. A guy who introduced himself as Craig from the Park, from somewhere up near Los Angeles. Said if you'd heard any of Harrison's teenager stories you'd know who he was. Guys he'd talked to a lot in Mesa Arizona, about The Van, two of them made it out, introduced themselves. Said they were sorry they missed you. He'd spoken so much about you to them. And all the folks at the Phone Company. Stella and some of her crew. Me and Tonette. About sixty folks more or less. Neighbors of yours and some woman who'd bought his paintings recently. Quite a crowd.

It seems Harrison sent off a letter to a mortuary with all the instructions. Then he wrote to the out-of-town folks, to invite them all, sent out letters days before the deed.

Had everything set up, sent Nicky over to your friend Stella's. Then that night he called 911 and tied off.

Danny says he got called too. Maintains he drove up a minute before the paramedics arrived. We're letting it go at that. But he couldn't make it to the funeral. Called later and said how sorry he was. But he just couldn't wrap his head around saying goodbye.

They played lots of music. He Ain't Heavy, He's My Brother, Oh, Me, Oh My, you know—Lulu. Too Much Saturn, Not Enough Moon. And a really beautiful one called Pieces of a Man. You know how Harrison loved all his old stuff. Lots of music. All during the memorial. Beautiful stuff.'

God. She has to lower the letter to her lap and swallow the sobs.

'I read out a letter Harrison left for the service. About you being such a wonder in his life and how he was so proud of that, how now that he was free of these pains; his being so long without Vivienne, his wings should be sprouting and boy, was he finally going to fly.

I saved it for you.'

Christina drives over to Word of Mouth first thing once the sun is up. Sits idling The Van, waiting for Willis and his Escort to pull up. It feels very cold. The heater isn't making a difference.

He pulls up next to her and she slips from the high front seat and into his waiting arms. "Oh, Willis."

"I know, babygirl. I know." The sun hits the rim of her side-view mirror. Shines on her newly shorn hair. "My god. What's this?" Willis touches the nape of Christina's neck. Mourns, "Too many changes."

"With your hair like that you look a lot less like Viv."

"Maybe that was the idea." Christina touches the tops of her ears, "I don't know." *Just something from my list*, she tries to convince herself.

"You out at the house? Need any help? I can have these minions run things for a day or two, you need any assistance." He sets a cup of coffee in front of her elbows, a bowl of grits, the sugar canister and a crock of butter. "Eat." A command, stepping to the next table for the salt and pepper. "You're getting to be all bones. You know that?"

But Christina only pushes the steaming grits around in the bowl, digs divots and slices swirls with the melting butter, but never raises the spoon. It's the being someplace she's come for. Not food.

Christina stands at the door, twisting her house key on its ring, Willis behind her. Like a nervous relator on her first open house. Christina tries three times before he has to take the key from her and give it a go.

Willis lays a hand on her shoulder and maneuvers her to the sofa. Sets her down nice and gentle. "We need a plan here. No need walking from room to room without a plan of attack. Where can I find a pen? Something to write on?" She never knew he was a guy to make lists.

She points to the top of the TV. There. Pulls her legs up and huddles. "I never planted that tree for Harrison in the front. I've got to get that done." She tells herself: *It's paid for.* Three bedrooms and a big, empty backyard. Thinks about the kitchen with that clock and wonders, *what do you do with this much sadness?* Willis talks as he writes, "Garage. Kitchen…"

But Christina is reaching for the phone. Dials Gina. The baby answers, Terri, the one who kisses dogs. "Gimmie your mama, honey." She's exhausted. No more strength. Smiles thinly at Willis with his pen held on pause, waiting. "Gina? Yeah, it's me… Thanks. I'm glad. That was nice. I didn't know you went. That's sweet, pink lilies? How nice… Well, tell them pink's a fine color for boys. Sure. Good choice." She looks up and smiles at Willis; "Her girls thought of the pink lilies they sent for Harrison."

"…Yeah. Me and Willis. From Word of Mouth… A bit, but not long, I'm heading back out as soon as I do some stuff here." Christina touches her forehead, lowers her chin, "I know. Yeah… Listen, 'member that Lotto number you gave me? At the Outrage? I never took you out to lunch, did I? For a thank you?"

The girls run from room to room, and out the patio doors to the wide backyard. Gina's speechless. Shaking her head, and mostly getting out the single syllable, 'Gurrrl' in varying tones of disbelief.

Low and astonished, from the moment that Christina sets them all down on the couch and walks them through the night that she won. After that, handing Gina the keys started the kids running from kitchen to bedrooms to the garage and back to the couch. "All ours!" Little Tina zooms by and keeps crowing. Hugging Gina, then the couch, then the walls themselves.

On the boards she logs in but hesitates, her fingers over the keys. What to say? A heavy heart. She's made such a mess of things. Will they let her back in? Where will she go if they don't? Pictures herself as Janeway. Stoic, but resolute. That look. A shipwide announcement to be made. In command of her emotions. Doing what has to be done. A thought bubbles up from that image of her hero, tempered by the past week's events.

****

TulipAna: My family suffered a loss recently. Very hard. But I'm back now.

Then she logs off and sits back in the recliner til darkness falls once more.

She can't get herself to check the thread again all the next day. Fearful of an empty, sucking sound. The verification of being unaccompanied through this.

Christina is stubborn about it; self-fulfilled abandonment. But finally kicks herself to log in again. And she finds herself staggered by the amount of replies posted. Her tribe gathering to murmur a heartfelt condolence. A reaching out, a touching of hand after virtual hand. A sharing of this vaguely expressed news simply because she was one of them and had spoken up about a grief. The emails and DMs flood her inbox. Mr. Paris, back on course. Engines at full impulse; Engage.

For some reason it's so much easier on the boards. At Stella's, Christina can hardly endure the number of people who want to hug her. She knows where the disparity of emotions are coming from. Can feel the reason way back in the recesses of her brain. Glad to have the answer, no matter how out of reach it feels. Just knows this 'Real Life' stuff hurts so much more.

She gathers Nicky up in her arms, familiar warmth, that huge bundle of tortoiseshell, somewhat of a shield. They can't get over a cat this size. "Forty inches when he's fully stretched out." Daniel says, stroking Nicky's tail, his new friend it seems, "We measured."

Thank god, a new topic.

She presses Harrison's canvases on Stella. "They're yours. He was so happy that you bought the first one." Having settled the house on Gina and her girls, the canvasses seem to be in need of a similar divestment. Christina won't take no for an answer. Harrison's spirit, his echoes need to be free of Heil Street. Once and for good.

Daniel offers to take Nicky's box out to The Van for her. "If you ever need someone to talk to. Just let me know." He pats at the box, and one last scratch for Nicky, watches for an exposed tail before he slides The Van's side door closed. "I'm your man. No matter where you go." She loves him most because he knows not to try for a hug.

She reaches in The Van for something to write on from her bike bag. "Here's where I'm staying. Can you come over after work some day?"

"Sure, sweetie. Anything for you."

"Wait, what?" Daniel shakes his head and looks around at the place. The perfect coral walls and oak furniture. The mica lamp shades. Nicky in all his glory here.

Christina takes a deep breath in, hating to have this conversation but she knows this is one of the last things she'll need to have handled before what's next. "Half of the whole rent. For about the next year, but maybe longer." Scratches at the back of her newly exposed neck, enunciating, one more time: "Do. You. Want. To?"

Daniel raises both hands, weighing his options as he speaks. Right hand up, circling about the golden room, "Live in my hovel and be poor." Shifts, left hand; "Live here for half your rent if I can do a few 'assistant' things for you with mail and packages every once in a while." He grins. "You're evil… I like that." Says, "If it won't get any kinkier than 'assistant,' then hell yeah."

"Well." Christina winks. "There's cat duty, too. Nicky's got the leash. But that's only kinky the first time."

Daniel shakes his head, still in awe. "But, why me?"

How to explain? The world he opened up for her. Daniel turns in all directions in the little hallway, "It's like the frackin' Lotto. You know?"

She looks around at the tiny place. "Yep."

She shows him the bedroom, apologizing about no furniture in there, but Daniel doesn't care. This is too good to be true. "Wow." Seeing the little office and PC, the desk and little chenille loveseat. Aloud, he pictures a backgammon game set up on the ottoman. The dinner he'd cook for Marc here. "I mean—*Wow.*" Nicky pads up, a paw on Daniel's pant leg. *Mister. Mister. Hey, Mister?*

"Just go with the win." Christina advises.

She purchases a Road Atlas software package for all the states, and then with her list of addresses, proceeds to map the locations of the group. Beginning with the west coast. Char in Arcadia, Kirigami all the way up in Carmel, and Klingon #1 in Bakersfield, someone in Pismo Beach, Klingon #2 in Berkeley, it's doable. One state at a time.

The colors she chooses for the walls work well. And for a moment she knows she'll miss being here. But she's decided. Daniel has the other key. Knows which of her accounts to pay his rent into. And that's that. Maybe she'll be back. Maybe look into buying the whole plaza. The six apartments and the 4 shops below. She could arrange for any new tenant to be a grad student. Or a novelist.

Chapter Fifteen

T HEY CONVERSE FOR what seems like hours via Skype. With the camera off, two voices back and forth. The Doctor is in; a voice Christina thought she knew, but couldn't place. But FaeLight07, such a friend, just keeps saying, 'All the time you need. Honest'.

Christina keeps checking anyway. Still feeling like an invisible soul.

FaeLight07's reply, no matter how often it's broached, is a variation of, 'Just a second pair of eyes and ears in which to see you, my dear.' After being sworn to complete secrecy, under a penalty of death, FaeLight07 hears the whole debacle. Doesn't stop listening until she has to say it, "Christina?"

That stops things.

"How did you know my name?" Christina asks.

"It's me, hon, Jean." Saying the one thing that takes Christina by surprise, in all this.

"Wow. That's a surprise."

"Surprise? How?"

"I don't know. The fact that I recognize what you meant before, I guess."

They agree, they'll meet for coffee, at last. Before Christina heads out on the road. Jean signing off with, "One last time, in real life."

The box Harrison left her holds five items. Four hard drives, loaded with every song he ever collected. Music for days, as his brief note read. And a hat box full of family photos.

Chrissie,

I figured with you and the videos you've been dreaming of making some day, that this music was best left for you. Music for days. Because that's what you've given me by allowing me to be your dad. The pics are so you remember our silly faces.

—-Harrison

So now that she has roots dealt with. The only thing left to attempt is to try the wings. Teach herself the one thing she needs to learn. Knowing whatever it is, that it's somewhere ahead of her on the road. And she figures she'll kick things off with the west coast, about 900 miles to try and find it.

Christina dreams she's made it back. Before Harrison's

funeral. Didn't miss it after all. Got the chance to say her piece. A lucid part of her asks, if this *was* a dream, then why was he really dead?

Shifts time, as dreams do. She finds he's standing at his own grave. Pink lilies in her hand, she speaks up, reads off the beginnings of a song from his record collection.

But tears stop her from going on.

She's trembling there in front of all the dream-folks who made it to say goodbye, from so far away. Can't catch her breath and can't get any more words out. Her hands tight in fists. Tears take away another breath and she tastes chorine in her nasal passages, thinks she may well pass out.

Willis comes up to stand by her. Wraps a strong arm around Christina's quavering frame. Steadies her so she can continue. But she sets aside the song. Decides to say what was in her heart, this may be the last chance. "He was always one to talk about strength. Wasn't a strong man in many ways. Believed in grace under pressure, and asked that I learn and live that too. He was brave." Christina wakes. Sobbing. Ready to go now.

There are still some things at the apartment to clear cut and some things elsewhere to set in place at the same time. Then there's nothing else holding her here.

When she has The Van packed, the big spaghetti pot stowed, and the bike immobilized with probably too many tie-downs, she takes one last look around the apartment. Seeing for the first time what a great little place she's made it. How much sun comes into the two front-facing windows, the delicacy of the railed walkway. How the scale of the furniture fits the rooms.

The J/7 board is on her laptop. Anywhere she'll end up being. And what else is there now, but the board? She says goodbye to the little place with her final walk-through. Then gets on the road for real.

She makes one stop at Word of Mouth, on the way out of town for one last goodbye, giving Willis a big hug. He stands at the door, to walk her out for the last time, the door he's opened so often after hours to anyone who needed him to. Christina wipes her eyes, foolish. Slips something into his shirt pocket, asks him to read it at home, with Tonette.

As she heaves herself up behind the wheel Christina shifts in her seat. Eyes on the mirrors, like Harrison drilled into her, she tells him, "Get writing, you old reprobate, you."

Willis waves that away, "Yeah, sure. You take care of yourself, babe." Pats the side of The Van, like he's going to miss them both. Steps back and with hand signals, waves her out of the parking lot. Then he heads back in, to start up the day's prep work, Christina watching out her rearview. He won't get it till he gets home. Reading her note. Seeing her check.

Wings are fine for soaring, she tells herself. But if she can interact one-on-one with the 700-odd number of board members in a virtual online world, then it's time to try for an equal number of folks she can experience face to face. Traffic included. No more hiding. Real Life, no matter how scary.

So to this end, Christina rides out of town this time in full daylight. Not even 55 miles into it and she feels so exhausted, weary way out of proportion, and she yawns and yawns and wipes at her eyes like they'll never stop streaming. A stiffness between her shoulder blades grows; shifting and arching just won't alleviate it.

Just before the cluster of reservations that straddle Interstate 8, Christina makes a quick decision to veer off to the south, choosing to follow State Route 94 into San Diego. She likes the sign she read before coming up to SR-94 that says Interstate 8 was actually Old Hwy 80. It must be an omen, that the board is still with her. *Here's a whole thoroughfare going under a separate username.* She muses. The change in direction is her chance to be in the real world. Off route. All new. No pseudonyms on her map. How could she resist such a find?

She'd begin the trip in earnest down in San Diego. To see *the Big Neon Sign* someone on the board had suggested, that hangs above the road in a section of town. Art deco, from the 1930's, they think. Suspended over a street to denote the neighborhood, supposedly it reads 'Normal Heights'. Seemed a good place to start. Maybe she'll photograph it. Start a new hobby.

She halts way before her first planned rest stop. Miles early. So much for her bid for 'Christina in reality'. Living *with* the world. She has to confess to herself that she's just plain knackered. Coffee does nothing but make another stop necessary to contend with its rental. She can barely keep her eyes open. *How do folks do this? Every day of their lives?*

She doesn't realize it's a reaction to leaving El Centro, her little town and inhabitants. That's the issue, seeing it all recede in her rearview mirror to drop away forever under the horizon as she rolls on and on westward.

Eventually, she doesn't care how real folks do it. Christina realizes she needs to lie down for a while. At mile 67 or so, with a quick glance in the mirror and several nervous taps on the brakes, she's slowed down enough to pull onto the berm without feeling like she's driven off the road and into the brush. Left the music on while consulting her maps, but no, unless she missed it, there's no rest-stop.

Oh hell. Christina! You've got a bed anywhere you want one. All you have to do is park and draw the curtains. Stupid girl. Get some sleep. And she sets her travel alarm for 4 p.m. It's that easy.

Two hours into her nap there comes a sharp rap on one of the windows, and the van is rocked like a semi has just swooshed by doing eighty-five. Another rap, this one more than just a stray rock kicked up by a passing big rig. Christina sits up in a panic. She's incorporated the rapping into a dream, as a knock at her door, an officer come to tell her about Harrison.

"Anyone in there?" Stern. And just a little pissed. *What's going on?* she wonders. She sets her feet on the floor, hunched up. Pulls the curtain aside and sees a State Trooper. Reflective glasses and cropped black hair. Frowning. And the only thing that comes to her as she scrambles up and steps out onto the road is Harrison's story about the couple he bought the van from. Drug mules. The punch line being: 'Honest officer, if I had known it was hazardous to my health, I never would have lit it up in the first place.'

"You realize you're just a hop skip and a throw from the U.S.-Mexico border, don't you Miss?"

She nods. She does now.

Brushing her hair back Christina tries looking helpful. Hoping the marks from the pillow she sees on her arm aren't all over her face too. He asks. "Where you headed?" They stand with the van's sliding door ajar. A living room open to the neighbors.

"A trip up the coast, San Diego, then up about fourteen stops or so." He's looking past her into the van. "Maybe get as far as the Oregon border..." She knows she's babbling. "State Beaches... Hostels..." running out of words. He's eyeing her maps on the driver's seat. Lets her words die down before reaching into the van and tapping on the spaghetti pot, glances back at her.

Christina opens it up, revealing a bottle of detergent and ten pairs of undies and a handful of bras rolled tight and snug. Forget the protocol for search or seizures. She unrolls nearly all of them to show how innocent it all is, shakes each one out and smiles, just wanting to be back on the road.

It's a few tense moments until he's certain of no illegals. No dope. And she promises the trooper and herself she'll only sleep at rest stops and designated camp sites from here on out.

He lets her go. On her way with a short lecture about young ladies traveling alone. That it's wise to have her passport with her like that. "And your van is a beaut." He should know, he'd opened up enough of it searching for 'what-not', as he very kindly put it.

"Quite a ride." Nothing else to search or destroy, serve or attach, "You gotta be sure to stop at Rincon Point, just shy of the Ventura, Santa Barbara county lines."

"Oh?"

"The ocean." He nods to himself more than her, taping his thick thigh with his citation book. "Nothing like this place."

He smiles. Waiting for her to tie back all the blackout curtains, and uses stiff important hand signals to guide her as Christina nervously maneuvers back onto the road.

On the highway again, keeping to a steady sixty-five mph, not refreshed at all, Christina can only shake her head and note to herself: real life. *Shit*.

She's so dumb. Didn't think to ask where the next rest stop might be. God, being this tired sucks.

A day later she stops at the Nite & Day Café. Coronado Island, Silver Strand State Beach.

"What will it be?"

A sailor orders. "A cheeseburger."

"Fries with that?"

"Nope."

The sailor steps to his left to pocket his change and a family moves up in unison, "What will it be?"

She can't believe it's 1:46 in the morning and folks are lined up like it was noon. Christina stands back and tries to decide to pig out, no one knows her here, it's not like anyone would know if she succumbed. The menu board, up on the wall, is calling to her. But by the time she's actually reached the register she's calmed down tremendously. "What will it be?" She orders the Greek chicken salad and a side of humus. Tea instead of diet soda.

She's been thinking about what the trooper said the day before. A young lady alone on the road—wonders if Harrison sent the guy to her in some fashion? *Could be*. That circles her mind the whole time she sits in The Van and eats her salad, sips her tea; this thought leads to her opening her laptop and asking Char and Jean to come along.

Luckily, everyone's awake and willing to chat. On a three-way Skype they plan where to meet up.

Come morning, Christina sits out on a canvas chair and stares at the water. The Van parked at her back. She connects to the Wi-Fi that the beach offers, logs into the boards and wonders aloud why she ever thought to undertake this trip without friends in the first place.

To pass the time she regales those online with tales of

the Trooper politely going through her undies.

TulipAna: What if I keep doing dumb things like that?

Klingon#1: Then you'll have more funny stories to tell when the trip is over, or a lot of scars you can bore us with.

TulipAna: Should I change my mind? No one's really out there waiting for me.

Klingon#1: I resemble that remark. I'm someone.

Klingon#2: One mistake doesn't mean the trip is doomed. Changing your mind means you'll miss out on seeing all of us as you come up the coast.

TulipAna: I'm really tired.

crAZy4J7: One day I want a trip like yours, be my hero, show the way.

LargeMarge: Take a day. There's no hurry. Look everything over. GET SOME SLEEP! Then make a decision. We want to see you, but the choice's yours.

TulipAna: I'm really, really tired.

Klingon#1: You can rest when you're old… And on that note, time for my nap.

There's Cal State Long Beach, if nothing else. Christina knows how to get there. She could stop and make plans from that hotel she stayed at when she first visited Char. Sure, she could breathe well there. Get some sleep. Feel brave enough to go on. Or tell the girls, nah, never mind. Better not.

Chapter Sixteen

"Baby steps, Christina." Jean had said that first time they talked. She knows.

Tricking herself into taking another and another step farther away from her actual life. Because that's what it feels like Christina needs right now. Baby steps. This trip is supposed to be a healing thing. And day by day, she confesses, "I only feel more bruised."

The drive on Interstate 8 surprised her, all that beauty in those pre-dawn shadows. Char is still up the coast, but Jean made it. Christina got her a rental, because she promised her one if Jean decided to come along. The coastline winks, a glimmer of water and dunes in and out of sight as the miles roll by. They'll be in Huntington Beach by noon, if she's calculated right.

At their lunch stop Jean says, "The thing to do is just calibrate El Centro as mile one. And keep piling up the miles, to nine-hundred." Jean wants to chart exactly where she'll be coming from and how she'll make her way. Figures she'll be brave and stop to see someone, "From a long time ago. A whole other life. Before El Centro, folks called Buddy and Regina." Jean pictures bringing some flowers and fruit; they haven't spoken in such a long time.

This time the drive is all the way up to Char's house in Arcadia, the green of the hilly neighborhood astounds both their senses after El Centro. Pine trees, emerald lawns, shiny bushes with the thickest of leaves. And the San Gabriel Mountains for a back yard. "How can anyone have this much green all the time?" Jean asks. "And I thought the beach was the wonder to experience."

Christina knocks. Nervous. But well-rested and willing. In her other hand she grips a bag of green apples and a hunk of cheddar cheese from a corner grocery in the town she just drove through, Sierra Madre. It was a stop on Christina's list. The place where they filmed the original Invasion of the Body Snatchers, The Fog, K-Pax (a favorite of Harrison's) and parts of Dude, Where's My Car?

Char's sister answers and calls behind her, "Char! It's Jean!"

And there Christina is again, smiling at a girl it feels like she's always known.

Char says "Oh, god, I nearly forgot, Harrison sent a letter or two here. While I was recouping. Rita? Where're those letters?"

"I got them." Christina tells Char, "I think you were still in the hospital. Rita sent them."

"Oh sure. But—" A hand comes out to touch her. "He sent more. Rita?"

The three women walk out to a park a few blocks from Char's house. Jean moves to the sidewalk's edge. And neither of them says anything.

They sit under the brilliant green of a spreading oak, on a picnic table that's dappled in its shade. Set their feet on the bench part of things. Jean is circling, exploring the greenery and making soft sounds of discovery to herself.

Christina selects the thinnest one of the letters to read. Not at all sure she wants the thickest one opened at all. Let alone opened in public. But she does, resting the pages on her knees under the tree's shade. And begins reading.

'…Remember how after she was gone, I was working that one site where they'd just put that new vault in? That corner right near the Kentucky Fried Chicken and for months all we'd eat was the buckets of the stuff I'd bring home after work. Sitting on the patio? You swearing I needed to be hosed off outdoors? You weren't gonna let me in till I stopped smelling like a sewer.

How the sun would be beating down and that family of hummingbirds flocked around the patio, under the eaves? After the chicken, how I got the hosing, then you made me sit in the Jacuzzi? Boy was that great times or what? You were always a great kid, Christina, I never deserved any better than you. Did I tell you I sold another piece? Yeah.'

Four days before he did it; Christina's checked the date stamp on this one. He was writing to her nearly up to the end. Char stays silent. Just a solid, quiet presence next to her; tears drop on the corner of the letter. Christina reads every word through it all.

'…I guess I could go down to a Xerox place. Take some copies, then email them to you. So you can see what's been falling out of the old man's brains, other than the brains, of course.'

He'd drawn a smiley face here. And Christina touches it with her forehead, holds it close for just a second, then lets the page fall from her hand. It's too much. She can't do it anymore. It's just too hard. She has to let it go. She *has* to.

Jean leans to retrieve the page and sets it on the bench. Waiting.

But then, after the tears, Christina reaches for the page and folds it up right. Creases it and slides it back into the envelope. Then she slips the envelope into her bag with the others that Rita handed over. Three more letters sent that same week.

"Rita set them aside until I was out of the hospital, then with the silence on the forum board and the emails not responded to, we forgot about them. Your post about family problems seemed to mean, 'Stand back. Don't intrude'."

So the letters had waited.

"I thought: she's back home. Whatever was happening you were there in El Centro. Dealing with it." The shame in Char's eyes looks like they'll never forgive herself for not sending them on.

Jean calls, "Coms see this!"

"You gonna be okay?"

"Um-hum."

"Can I do anything?"

"Nuh-uh."

Christina will need to find a place for these letters. Char and Jean are thin-lipped. No one's saying anything. There's the box she'd picked up while she was down visiting Char that one time. That beautiful find that Christina knew was hers the moment she saw it, before she even knew she'd be needing it for treasures like this.

Leo Carrillo State Beach. Mile 110, give or take. Jean re-reads the State Park brochure aloud to them, about the tribe that once inhabited this area, as she sits in The Van. Char's decided to try to hike out to the beach: *They enjoyed games, singing, dancing, gambling and trading with other tribes.*

The drive up the Pacific Coast Highway from the 210 Freeway helped everyone's tears abate. Christina was left thinking she'd be alright now. Thinking, *I can do this. I can go the whole way.* As chatty as these two are on the boards, here in The Van they both keep pretty quiet. Christina notices that.

She still hasn't read all the letters yet.

Christina listens to Char who's explaining, "You can't

park right on the sand here, the camping spaces are hill-ward, on the land side of the highway." So she follows the pointing and drives along a ways up in the scrub on the hills. Christina's booked a camp site for a five-day stay. But she hadn't understood that the only access to the beach side, with those rocks and the wooden steps to the various small cove areas like in the photos online, was via a dank and smelly underpass.

The footing is slippery but the other beachgoers are in such high spirits about the great-looking day that Christina's own hesitant steps, picking a way through the clammy passageway, catch some of their delight and now Char is considering climbing that rock herself.

Christina chose this stop because of the brochure. Reading about the Chumash people, their elaborate cave and rock art. How they were marvelous artisans; their basketry, how they lived here as far back as 6,000 B.C.

She wonders if anyone would find Harrison's work that far into the future. Wonders if anyone would care. And that leads her to ask Jean if she *should* care. Because these letters are waiting, and Christina's mind keeps on nagging her about being a big baby and not reading them.

Harrison's handwriting seems to be so alive on the pages that Christina's feeling that if she could turn fast enough, she'll catch him from the corner of her eye. She sits on the beach quilt they'd carried and reads, '*...it's nothing. I mean... it—it's something. Something that changed our, your life. See, it weighs*

on me and I want to be able to feel I've said it to you. To think I've finally got it off my chest...'

Christina flips the letter over and sets it under her thigh. Holds it tight there. Safe from her own eyes and Jean's, which are filling up and spilling over. Not wanting to know what's next. Knowing how it all ends. Char was climbing on rocks, off to their right. So it's just Jean, sighing, saying, "I'm really hating the thought of you, my little friend, having to deal with anymore." *Especially Harrison's ghost.*

But it has to be done. Jean exhales; a long, ragged breath. Witnessing. Listening to Christina read more, *'...The day your mom died. It's about that. I thought about letting you write me and tell me if you were up to this. I don't want to hand over anything you're not ready for. And believe me. Not knowing this won't hurt you in any way kiddo. If you're not up to it, it won't hurt you to skip knowing. Thought I'd cut you some slack, tell you to say the word or keep mum. And I'll understand... But, well. There's places I gotta be soon, so here goes...'*

"The old fart." Christina sits back. Has to grin. Though the waves are blurred and she knows the rest of the letter will have to wait till she's a whole lot stronger than today. But she finds herself unable to stop with her grinning now, and says out loud to the waves and the sky, and Jean, "If he wasn't dead already, I think I'd kick his scrawny ass about now for putting me through all this."

Before she puts the letter back in its envelope, she tries one more time. Risking how strong she might be after all. Jean's hand on her thigh helps.

'...I wanna tell you about this. Now's as good a time as any

and well, yeah. You need to know. You're a big girl now. So what it was, was... Well. I'm such a fuckin coward I should have told you this a long time ago. I'm bad on stuff like this though, you take one day at a time and don't get something done right then and then wham five years are gone and you still haven't said anything out loud. Even if every night you're going to sleep saying, I'll do it tomorrow. Tomorrow for sure.

Don't hate me okay. Whatever you want to think of me it'll all probably be true. But don't hate me for what I've been, what I am, still. Okay? Promise me? Here's the thing. The day your mom got in that car accident. Well, she was pretty mad when she got into her car. When she drove off. Steamed, so pissed I was glad she grabbed the keys and left. I couldn't take it anymore. We'd been fighting all day. Don't know if you remember. Don't know what you were doing. Even if you were in the house that afternoon, or what.'

And like father like daughter, Christina stops the letter there. Tucking it into the envelope she decides to go for a walk on the shore alone.

Harrison's letter has Jean's face burning. She tells Christina, "It's like he's cribbed from my own life." And looking out over the waves, she adds, "Don't read it if you can't."

As Christina gets up to move away, Jean shades her eyes, scanning for Char. The tide is out and the biggest climbable rock swarms with kids and adults. "Hey! Lookit Me!" "Mom! Take a picture!" The sky is aqua blue.

All Christina can think to herself is, *tomorrow.*

'...Should know, if you were there or not, huh? Damn. Well, you CAN hate me for that one. For not knowing. You have my permission. Anyway tangents, sorry. So she drove off all mad as hell and not gonna take it anymore. And the reason I'm telling you is just to let you know we'd been fighting. And that's why Mom got out on the road that day. Why that truck hit her side on. Because of me. Because of me, begging her not to kick my sorry ass out. She seemed ready to give back the ring and after what I saw as seven pretty damn good years she wanted to shut it all down and, 'you go your way, buddy boy, and me, I'll go mine'.

The problem was, she wanted to take you too. Make my fine and beautiful life some hollow memory. So that's when I got into begging. Did you ever see any of that? Well, I did beg. One fine assed little beggar of a dude with Viv, always. And I guess this time she just couldn't take it anymore and it finally shoved her out the front door and into her car.

When the cops came to the door later, I thought she'd sent them. Wanting to kick me out then and there. For a moment when the guy took his hat off, rain dripping down his neck, I figured they're never that polite for an eviction—so what the fuck's up here? And I confess right here to you now, Chrissie, too much of me was glad when I found out the real scoop.

That cop must have thought, shit, he's stoned. Walked me out to the squad car and let me sit in front, turned on his heater, way up high, and we were off to the hospital where they made me ID her body.

I guess you can look at this like she got so pissed that she got herself in the path of a red-light jumper. Or maybe now that you know all the begging stuff—now maybe you might think: He drove her out to meet up with it.'

Chapter Seventeen

'*B*ad luck all the way around. For you the most.

But like I said. This's something I felt you had to know. Because I'm doing my best here to get it all out on the table for you to be the judge of my sorry character. You're the one who's mattered to me all these years. You're the family I kept begging for that day.

And I'm so dammed sorry that all the begging lost you your mom. For that I truly am, baby.

You deserved so much of a better life than the one I rigged you up with. Please forgive me. Please see it wasn't my plan all along. Like your mom used to say, "Crap happens all the time. You gonna clean it up or what." Here's me trying to do just that.'

There are a few lines more, but Christina just hasn't the heart for it right now.

Char tells a couple of lame jokes after dinner. And they all laugh as expected. But for Christina it dawns on her that it isn't really her own laughter; that has fled. Crushed under a guilt deep in her chest. A live thing, that turned and turned and couldn't settle. Like she's seeing herself sitting next to the laughing girl, feeling it all happen outside herself.

'I hope your trip along the coast is great and that the towns you stop in remind you of how much you miss your old man, because I sure miss you at every step I take, here in poor old El Centro. You're not missing a thing here. That's for sure darling.

P.S. Stumbled on an oldie moldie that just took my breath away. You'd love it. Gil Scott Heron. Made me want to sit down and write you this letter. The mixed tape, labeled Birthday Jam from Mr. Moore. Haven't thought of Mr. Moore since my time up in San Francisco, before I even met your mom. But god bless him he was one great mixer of tapes. The one this Heron's on, it's a beaut. Song called 'Pieces of a Man'.

The albums and tapes and all are getting loaded slow but sure into the software and now I'm putting them all over into the extra hard drive you got me. You'll get the drive and some disks I make and a master list of all the tunes as soon as I get it all together.

Life's good when I don't look too deep into the crevices.

Your loving dad. Keep well baby.

Harrison.

The next morning the three decide to go for a hike, beachside, so they plan up a picnic. Jean volunteers to drive up to the next grocery stop, bring back a roasted chicken, fixings for a fruit salad and more wine. "Jean," Char asks, rummaging in The Van for something. "Where's the backgammon set?"

Christina offers her small camp stove, "I'm willing to cook up some satay chicken. We've got the fixings for a marinade, if you're interested." She sees the verbiage of the park's brochure in her mind, about the tribes in the area and grins: *They enjoyed games… and trading with others.*

Char explains stuff to Christina, "We were three and a half hours apart. Drive time. The Palm Springs route was the easiest. We'd meet up in between, or once in a while one of us would drive the whole way, spend some time at the other's house. Usually down here."

Christina asks, "So you have to come the farthest?"

"Pretty much how the relationship is set up, yep."

They've walked past Sequit rock, the beautiful one with the arch, that creates a walk-through cave at low tide. Up past North Beach, all around them calf-high grasses grow, whipping about in wild dance in the strong breezes from the highway to the east. Their goal is Staircase Beach, the far northern portion of the beach side of the park. Char and Christina take turns lugging the wheeled cooler and carrying the compact camp stove. And Jean contends with the three folded canvas chairs. A wind's come up from the shore now too, and Christina's glad she's got a hoodie on.

Finally, they get to the little cove, just a perfect spot for a picnic. The three all flop onto the sand and start preparing the site, as if this is something they've done time and time again.

Christina files this feeling away; how fast friends can fit into her life. How easy something she held herself back from could be, to approach and tame. *What was I thinking, not doing this sooner?* And the trio, camp stove lit, sit back on the blankets to talk and talk...

"Oh, the dream of school's leaving me." Char tells her when they go walking on the hard wet sand. "I can see that every day of the week. This wasn't meant to last."

"And that's okay with you?"

Char's reaction to that as she ponders, watching Jean's figure nearly gone from sight up ahead, heading to the parking lot; for the food run, stings. Christina didn't think it would, but it does. She feels Char's sorrow like it's her own. A loss plays right across Char's face. And Christina, seeing it, clicks things together all in a flash. She wonders if Char thinks that's hidden, or if she knows it's out on display.

"Wanna talk about it?" It's all she can think to ask.

Char pulls her phone from her jacket, flips up a photo. Christina reaches for the phone, holds it closer to be sure. She had no idea. Char and Jean. "There's only one happiness in life. And that's to love and be loved. School's minor to that." Char's got the phone again, flips to more and more pictures. She shows Christina: "Thanksgiving at her house last year, talk about a long-distance relationship. I drove all the way to El Centro for her. You ever see two people smile like that who weren't loved and loving? Sure she's old enough to nearly be my mom's age, but still. It was some real stuff we had."

Char's gray shirt reads Kotzerbue Alaska, Jean's hand resting on her thigh. Bliss in both their faces. And the two of them, like magnets, leaning in toward each other, their heads just about to touch. Smiles on the pair of them. Proud, happy, at something the two of them created together.

"Length of time or distance of the trip really were just small parts of that equation."

Christina uses her palm to shade the screen so she can study their photo. She's guessing it's a Thanksgiving where Jean's whole family's shown up, so that extra tables had to be set up out on the patio. Christina's mind goes wandering, picturing it all right in front of her. Probably too many people in the kitchen to maneuver. She pictures how it was surely loud, too. Laughter, the kind that keeps rolling in from the living room. Everyone sitting after the meal around a fire pit in the warm backyard. Talking. Waiting for some space to appear in their bellies for the next piece of pie. So much festiveness in the air.

Char looks at the photo too, comes up with another smile like the one there in her hand, "Yeah, it may be on its way out for us, but it's been there. And that's what stays. The fact that one time, it *was* there. School… school's not even close to that."

Christina needs to know why. What was the reason for a no-go situation when it comes to love? To her mother driving out into the rain, to Harrison left at the house, willing to beg for as long as it took. "Too much distance to travel?"

"Too much happiness to let it survive." Char shades her eyes, looking up the beach again, but Jean's no longer in sight. "Not all of us can accept it when a sweepstake falls into our laps."

"Too much happiness." Strangers in Christina's dreams keep popping up too often not to be symbolic.

They've just walked out of a dream restaurant. A place like Willis', but it feels like down in Seal Beach. The sunshine has to be beach sunlight. All mixed up like dreams do to you. Her two friends kiss, and Christina looks away, down to their shadow, notices that the setting sun fills the space under their joined chins—where their bodies don't meet, throws a misshapen heart in the sand between them.

She's got a hangover from last night's wine.

Jean opens the window on The Van and Christina decides to lie down for a nap. The afternoon's taking too long to pass. And she has to do some thinking now. About how happy and sad Char was feeling, cycling through it all at the same time.

Night's fallen when she opens her eyes again. Christina lifts herself up on one elbow.

And then shuts her eyes again. Rolls back over and falls back into sleep.

The Trek's chrome spokes, strapped to the back of The Van

all these months, reflect the setting sun as Christina rests at a picnic bench at 5:30 p.m. on the twenty-seventh of June. Rincon Point, CA. The state trooper's dream spot. From her vantage point she looks for quite a ways in each direction, both northward and south. It's not El Centro, or a hop skip or a throw from the border. *That's* for sure.

Behind her, across the PCH highway, towers a steep bluff. Christina pictures herself up on that cliff, a blanket-sized wrap around her shoulders. The wind blowing her hair from her face. The sea crashing in waves below.

Shading her eyes, she makes out some type of pine trees and eucalyptus. Here at the picnic area, she rests from a walk along and back again on the wide swatch of beach; surfers and tide pools closer to the shore and other campers here on the parking area.

The sun warms the top of her hair as she sits on the table part of the bench, arms resting on knees, head bent… willing herself to open another of Harrison's letters; this seems like the place for one.

Even when it's like tearing band-aids off unhealed scabs.

Strangers with kids, and some with dogs, walk past, pausing, comment on The Van. Char and Jean have gone for a walk to see if there's a store anywhere near.

One woman, a wide bit of Madras-print fabric wrapped around her thin waist, a bikini top and an ample shade hat, stops and strikes up a conversation, running her hand along the side of The Van. She tells Christina, "Great color on the bike; I love that shade of maroon. Are you Kate?"

Christina confesses the bike comes along but really, she doesn't ride much now that she drives. "Sentimental more than anything…" she trails off and looks back down to her letter.

So the blonde ignores the fact that the question about her name got sloughed off. She leans against the bench and crosses her arms, talking to the ocean, like The Van is an eavesdropper.

"Worst thing I ever did in life, a bike run one May from San Francisco down to L.A. Five hundred and forty-something miles in a week." Christina gasps. Holds her hand to her chest and the blonde, she nods and enunciates, "Oh. My. God."

"You have got to be kidding." The letter's forgotten.

"Nope. For an annual AIDS Ride." She mentions the year.

Christina takes a second look at her, years after she and Harrison lost her mother this woman was riding down this coast. And now here they were talking. *She must have been near my age then.*

"I got to L.A., finished walking the 'We-Made-It' parade in my purple jersey, still have that by the way. Well, I up and left the bike at a Fat Burgers we stopped at, never even looked back. Slept for, I dunno, four days maybe."

Christina laughs when the woman slaps her own thigh and adds, "One thing I learned: my safe word from there on out: *Owww.*"

And the blonde offers to come by in the morning and join Christina for biking a short jaunt up into Carpentaria for breakfast. She points out the private beach to their right; telling Christina she's house sitting. "The trip to town's only two miles tops in each direction, I know a great place for huevos rancheros, it's like their tradition for this one place. Killer, the salsa will knock your eyes out." she assures. Then jokes when Christina hesitates, "and the trip back's all down-hill, North to South," her hand gesturing a map of California in the air, pointing *there* back to *here*. She says, "Call me Jules." Offers a hand, the one still warm from such a familiar touch on The Van.

"From where?"

The bike ride up the beach to Carpentaria had been decided against, once Christina found they could walk the railroad tracks all the way up. The pair are now halfway to breakfast.

"El Centro. Imperial Valley. You know it? I'd guess about three-hundred miles or so south and east." The distance, said out loud that way, makes Cristina wonder if she's even heard of it, so foreign sounding now that she's been to Crystal Cove and Silver Strand, Rincon Point and Torrey Pines.

"Nope. I stick to the coast mostly, and the Central coast at that."

"Warrants out in the other counties?"

And Jules laughs.

The breakfast, as advertised, is killer. And makes the walk down the beach back to The Van an easy stroll. Their strides match, the pace is slower. There's no hurry to part company and get on with other solitary things. Char and Jean, wherever they may be, it's okay not to know. The sun now near overhead, throwing sparkles into the water.

There's that echo deep in her chest, she sees it clear as day: Harrison in the kitchen, noticing something's changed, saying, "Where'd that tension go to? You're so mellow it's like you've been sneaking bong hits."

"I'm as tense as I've ever been." She'd protested. "Maybe more."

"Nope," letting Nicky climb his chest and settle for a snuggle under his chin. "You're a friggin' Yoga Master compared to when you were taking ads at the paper."

Where did that come from? Christina wonders as she inhales and shakes it off.

They walk and talk like they had planned this get-together. Knew each other instantly, or rather, recognized each other as old friends. Christina wonders if the day's been so comfortable because of trying to be a new person? Or because this new person she seems to be is too familiar to be faked? *Did I step into playing myself?* The role she's waited so long to be offered?

Maybe Char or Jean will know.

Three days later and they still haven't moved on up the coast. Mainly because a mention of barbecue recipes segues into an offer of kitchen privileges at the house Jules is pet-sitting for. Four dogs and a kitten. Now, the three of them sit in The Van as it rolls though Jules' guarded gate.

"So these were like moments of time, using clips from the show to convey new and different emotions? New circumstances and scenarios?" Jules asks, hearing about vidding from Char as they eat.

"Sure. A song that has a story to it already" Char's explaining, while sipping white wine. "Or a scene from the show set to a piece of music, something evoking the heart of the scene in lyrics."

Jean adds, "The other option is the one I like best."

"What's that?"

"When you find a song and all the right clips and come up with a new moment, where it's not about the show. About some moment in time. It's about *my* moment in time."

"Have many of those, do you?" Christina asks.

But Jean knows better, "This was maybe the best barbecue I've ever tasted."

Jules wipes her fingers and Christina bows, telling them, "A friend taught me this. Though it's just a marinade for chicken, it's more a grill than a barbecue. Now *his* stuff, smoked meats and real sauce—peppery. Cornbread and spicy fries. You know? Knock your eyes out. Talk about good barbecue."

Chapter Eighteen

"EACH OF YOU just take a bedroom." In this rambling house, Jules insists it isn't a problem. Jean and Char share a look, yawn and then head up the stairs off the kitchen. Christina waits in the living room, staring out on the waves she can hear through the sliding French doors. Too much in her head to entertain thoughts of lying down.

She and Jules talk late into the night, once Christina has confessed to this near stranger about the Lotto win. Even letting her know the prize amount, something only Harrison had known. "…so what is it you're so damn afraid of?" Jules yawns as she asks.

"Life." Christina removes the soft kitten, lounging on the sofa back, inches from her neck, "But I think, 'If I take this new stuff as slow as possible I might be able to sneak up on it and wrestle it into submission'." She looks into Jules' eyes. "You with me?"

"Gotta be. I've never seen anyone in needs of a side-kick

more than you are."

Christina looks up and sees all the art on every wall. A paper-mâché walrus head, she remembers the silver goat in the foyer, the murals of the whales along the patio wall. The two of them talk and talk, way into the night.

"See… It works like this, baby—" Smoke rails up from Jules' cigarette, catches the golden of the sunset. Twists and dances in that light. "You walk down a street and keep falling into a hole you never noticed was there. Things happen. Lessons are learned. Then one day you're walking down the same street and you see the hole. But shit, you manage to fall in it again anyway.

More days pass, more lessons learnt. What's this? One day you walk down that street, see the hole this time, and walk around it, for once you don't fall in—"

Christina's nodding. The she notices she's also grinning, and can't help watching the smoke spirals. And now she knows this is some damn special night here. She blushes at that, looks down, studying her own hands. Not the lines, but she's noticing her cuticles are healing. *When did that start?*

"—there's other holes up ahead, but you damn sure recognized that old one. No more for you, buddy—not *that* hole, you're not falling in there again."

This close to daylight, Christina can almost see her future.

Their kiss is a light one. Has, it seems, nothing at all to do with sex. And that confuses Christina. *Am I supposed to feel something?* Then it hits her—a delayed reaction, and there, at the nape of her neck the heat catches; streams down her spine and rests at her tailbone, hesitates before turning inwards and setting just about every part of her on fire.

Oh, my god, she thinks.

"Sorry. It just seemed… okay, to do that." Jules' eyes slant up, smiling. Her hand still on Christina's cheek. "Oh, god." She's read the look on Christina's face. Sees this might be her first kiss, maybe ever. "Oh, wow. Really." Removes her hand and sits back, "I'm not naturally a lecher. Are you okay?"

Christina sits back too, her mouth slightly open, wondering if she should share the fact that her fingers are tingling. What's the protocol for this type of realization? "Umm—" Clears her throat and says the first thing that comes to her mind. "I've been on the road for days. Can I use your shower?"

Jules is lying on the bed on her stomach, reading a magazine. Her head faces the footboard and one of the skinny cats sits balanced on the flat of her back, licking first one paw then the other. When Christina comes in from the bathroom she looks to the cat then decides to sit on the floor at the foot of the bed. Rests her back up against the mattress.

Jules reaches down over the side and the cat makes a long jump past them both and trots off: *things to do. Gotta go. Later.* It's a stretch, but Jules seems up to it, she shifts and Christina feels a pat, friendly, no threat, on the top of her wet hair. "Hey there."

In Bakersfield, a hearty bear hug meets her at Klingon_01's front gate. He ushers her indoors, and like with Char and Jean, they've fallen into conversation, "…It's easy when you're as skinny as you are." Christina tells Buddy when they meet up, a dog-leg to the east, inward from the coast.

"What?"

"I've got more weight to carry around. Is all. It's not as easy."

"Christina, how much do you weigh?" that stops her, making it abundantly apparent she has no idea for sure. She bikes so many places now because she wants to see the beauty around her; see the view from the highest hill. She wears what she feels like because she can, not because she can finally fit into it.

She glances over to Jules, who's mute, just watching this exchange. "You gonna post this on the board?" Christina jokes.

"I got a daughter, Cinda. Hates a lot of stuff. Me for instance, but other things, too, even about herself. I just don't get it." His eyes grow sad and for a moment he seems a lot older than she knows he is. But Christina pulls him out of the funk when she changes the subject and asks about visiting the other Klingon next, "So I was wondering, should I take the upper route?" points to the up and over blue lines on her outspread map, 140 plus miles to Pismo Beach, but just a fraction of it along the coast.

"I can backtrack, that's about a hundred and twenty-five miles back to Ventura, but at least the hundred more miles from there are all along the water."

Buddy nods, wise move, "I wouldn't miss any of the ocean if I could help it."

But he refuses to listen when she tells him she wants to start right back after dinner. "I'll wrestle the keys from you if I have to. Seriously, if you don't want to sleep in the guest room, then go stay in your van, but no more driving today. And that's an order."

Buddy cooks a great Surf and Turf meal for them, steak meets lobster. He promises the house specialty; a garlic and herb butter for the shrimp and strip loin topped lovingly with a crumbled feta cheese. "We can crack open a bottle of Viognier, it's a nice fruity wine, arid as Bakersfield. Perfect with the wild rice."

"No wine." Christina says, "I tried that. Once is enough. Woke up with my first hangover. Thought it was the same as a head cold—I expected it to last a full week."

Buddy looks to Jules, who shrugs, and he croons, "Oh, you babies." He's lifted the steak from the grill, "Now we just wait for it to rest. Like the cook."

"Oh my god." Jules sighs at the aroma of the meat on the platter, "How long do we have to wait?"

He slaps at her hand with a dish towel. "A minimum of five minutes, I like to cover it at five and go for an extra three while it's under foil." He winks, "Gives me time to get chased around the table once or twice." He points to his *kiss the coo*k apron. Rolls his eyes and laughs. "The extra three doesn't do a thing for the steak, by the way."

They stand at the door, loath to leave, and thank Buddy all

over again. Christina hugs like it's Harrison back for a brief moment, nearly squeezes all the air out of him. And Buddy lets her. When she asks for the recipes from both of last nights' dishes Buddy beams, more than happy to oblige the request.

"Do me a big favor while you're making your way back to Ventura. You've seen the road on the way up here so you can do this with your brain instead."

"Name it."

"Look in your mirror every few miles. At the rest stops twist it to you and take a good long look. See who this lovely girl is, that I see here, Christina."

She ducks her head, like the words are blows. "Fell into that one, didn't I?"

"Trust me on this one. It'll do you good. I promise."

But on the ride back down to the coast Christina ignores the mirrors. Doesn't even notice her own shadow when she makes the rest stops. Thinks she's still fat because when she looks down she sees her shirts and tops not her shoes. Not figuring it out that that's all boobs, not a Buddha belly. That really, she's looking at herself through *Viv's* eyes, and that'll never work.

No matter how Jules tries, Christina continues her bad eating habits of only feeding off her past.

"Ana." Christina taps her chest, not knowing why that name's come out of her mouth. Why she's even willing to sit for this palmistry reading. Jules waits outside, on the beach boardwalk.

Shara, the woman nearly swallowed in scarves, nods, then says something weird, "Today, maybe." Christina doesn't risk asking her to repeat it. "Okay, let's see what we've got here."

Christina leans in too, like looking in and hoping to see Koi in a pond, hardly breathing at all.

"I see you're some type of storyteller. But not a traditional one. You do things with electronics? Computers? That type of work?" Like looking into a deep well, Shara leans over Christina's palm and peers.

Christina grins, *yeah?* "Never thought about it. Right now I'm unemployed."

"Well, there's your path. Building, design, storytelling at that level." Shara points to just left of center on the palm and both the women look like it's neither of theirs. "Here. Fate and Mercury lines. But an air palm for sure. Maybe that's the reason for the pseudonym."

Christina regards the lines. Scratches her hair with her free hand and ignores the bit about being *Ana* today. Okay then. She wants to retract it from Shara's warm hold, hand her a ten. Get away from there. But Shara's gauging the lengths of Christina's fingers now, touches the tip of her index finger, then goes on talking, a few other points.

"See, you've got Jupiter, good fortune, retreating for some reason into the background, or it's somehow damaged." She waggles the pinky, "A longer little finger. You express yourself extremely well." She looks up for verification, Christina flashes on the call from Beverly, back at the Outlook.

Next Shara runs her finger along that earlier line again. "The strong Mercury."

"Good to know. I may look into that." *What the heck.*

But now she's tapping the side of Christina's hand, "Not to mention a few trips in the mix."

At that, Christina does pull away, but this doesn't faze Shara, who simply removes her own hands from the table, secrets them in her lap, but continues leaning over that well, gently saying, "Nevertheless, for the most part, very self-abnegating. You've gotta stop that soon—*Ana.*"

Cambria Youth Hostel: With the music up so loud that morning, once Christina actually registers the sign reading, *Welcome to Cambria*, the pair roar right past the Main Street exit off of Scenic Highway One. And she knows she'll have to make a U-turn somewhere up ahead.

To her right she catches what seems like twelve seconds of village rooftops before it looks like the entirety of Cambria is behind her. They're so intent on turning, and that seems to mean traversing the highway into oncoming traffic, that something called Burton Drive gets past her before she slows enough; and there to their left they find Moonstone Beach Drive to make the turnaround.

Two miles of back-tracking and another lane crossing brings her to Main Street again, then it's trust in the map because she seems to be driving not only up and up and up, but back the way she just came from on the highway.

It has to be here somewhere. Christina tries not to watch the sky and trees and the general captivating feel of it all, and concentrates instead on street names. Rolls down her window and the scent of pine pushes into the van. Bridge Street, Bridge Street. And it's another two miles before she parks and pulls the break. Now so turned around there's little chance she'll find her way back to the highway without a guide.

Two kids are lounging on the lawn in front of the hostel. A girl who looks about ten and her younger friend, a towheaded boy of about eight.

"Hi." Christina calls, pulling her bag from the passenger seat. The girl smiles, moves off her blue lawn chair to the white picket fence. Her sidekick follows suit.

"You work here?" Christina jokes to the girl, while pushing her sunglasses up onto her curls and yawning.

The boy answers. "Nah. That's my sister, Pilar. We're guests. From Southern California." The emphasis on Southern. "I'm Samuel." He holds open the gate like a gentleman.

The fully equipped kitchen is open to guests. And it's Pilar who hangs on the edge of Jules' footboard and asks, "Do either of you girls cook?"

It's Christina who answers, after stowing her bag under the bed. And Pilar and her brother both take a hand and, giggling, drag her into the common area kitchen.

A double bed and 2 built-in bunks in this one room. Christina drops Jules back down on Rincon Pt. so it's only her here now. Plenty of space to spread out if she wants to. And that seems just a bit weird. A touch off-kilter. But she's trying hard to deal with it.

The kids help take her mind away from turning right around and going back for Jules, away from asking her to join in on these nine-hundred miles. Basically, for Christina to take the chance of her life.

"Do you miss your sister?" Pilar asks as the short ribs are simmering in the crockpot, slathered with barbecue sauce over a whole chopped onion.

Samuel offers, "I'd never leave my sister somewhere and keep going. I'm here cause the universe knew she'd be here." And Pilar offers a curtsey to that, head dipped, shyest of grins.

Before she turns to Christina and wonders, "What's it like having a blonde in the family? Do you ever get jealous?"

Christina dreams that Jules is standing at the window, silhouetted, dark against the sheer linen curtains. In the dream, she remembers cooking with the kids in the hostel's wide kitchen, the pots and pans making ringing noises up to the broad ceiling. All the laughing, and now, as she sleeps, finding Jules at the doorway, watching them. She's in a pose now; a watching, waiting tilt to her profile.

Though the dream-room's filled with grays and damped-down night tones—Christina has trouble making things out, not like normal dreams that've come before. That's what fools her into thinking she's not dreaming; in Christina's dreams any girl she finally kisses has hair of the brightest auburn.

So she lies still, curled on her side, watching Jules through the hostel room's shadows. But she doesn't turn her head from the window. So Christina knows that the next move, if any, well, it'll be up to her.

She thinks on things and comes up with two solutions. Break the spell by rolling over to face the wall, pulling herself into an even smaller ball, her hands giving up the prayer and reaching to shield her heart.

Or reach out to her. A woman who wants to be touched, who lets Christina into her bed for a reason.

Behind her, the dream-Jules hears her sigh. Hears a whisper, from Christina, soft and muffled. She doesn't turn from the window, only asks, "humm?"

The sky isn't bright enough to show through the gauzy curtains yet, but the two of them can tell the night's over. Even without the dream's dawn letting them know.

That following morning, Christina's voice rises up from the bed, "It's so late I think it's already tomorrow." Forgetting for a second that Jules isn't there to shift under the covers, waiting for her to add anything more; Christina's body feels the tow of no other's movements where there should be two planets in mutual orbit. Still, she speaks to the empty room: "You're nowhere like my last—my James. I—it felt right—kissing you." From the sound of Christina's voice now fully awake and listening—waiting—comes no reply. So she adds her own, a statement of recognition, "Funny. I never knew there'd be such a difference."

There are steps, soft on the hallway floor beyond her door, but they don't come towards the bedroom. The bathroom door closes with a soft *click*, it hangs over Christina in the decreasing dimness.

From there she recalls last night's board game. Remembering Pilar and her brother, Samuel. Something—nearly a whole idea—comes to her fully formed. She reaches for her notebook now that the sun's up enough to shine in through the windows.

Flips from one half-finished project to the other, like a shore bird with too many worms wriggling so close by.

The notions for the game just pour out, nearly faster than she can get them down. Maybe, she thinks, there can be a TV, with video that players can watch. And the next level is earned if, after the TV show the littler brother, no *Little Sister*... she scratches something out and scribbles down more. *Yeah. Yeah.*

So what happens when the player watches all the videos? Or wins at keeping her safe? Christina taps her pencil against her tooth.

How dumb. It hits like a wave splashing on her feet, nearly makes her jump. *A second little sister.*

The sky's the limit.

Every morning that Christina wakes next to no Jules, she takes a deep breath and pictures them together, for as long as it takes to solidify in her mind. Once the image stays, then she starts writing, her notebook never far from her hand. This time it's for a video list. If she breaks down and buys all the disks, the full seven seasons of Voyager, she can take things a step at a time and build a list of all the clips. Who's in each scene? Is it a two-shot, an extreme close up? An action shot of the ship? Maybe a separate list of all the aliens, one that you can cut across to from the major list. *So it'll need a way to link the two lists. There's got to be a way to do that.* She writes and writes and writes. It doesn't matter that the sun's coming up now. Christina can sleep later.

She can post on the forum that once it's done; anyone can use it for making their own vids.

Finally, San Francisco.

Christina's broken down and asked Jules to meet her. Though technically they're at the hostel out on the bluff at Point Reyes, the beach names make her head swim: *Sculptured, Limantour, Agate, Santa Maria, Wilacat.* What she wouldn't give to be mailing off a letter from Agate Beach back to Harrison.

"Sure you may have some bucks, but look at you— you're living like a refugee. I bet if you could you'd turn the sun off every day. Tell yourself, 'who needs light. I'm fine here in this dimness. It's just me'."

"I'm working on it." Is all she can counter with.

Christina isn't looking to change the way Jules seems to think she needs to.

"Man. Even your creations are getting ignored."

But she has to draw the line there, Christina holds up her notebook. Evidence of some kind. But even she can see it's maybe less than it seems, now that Jules is here to weigh it in her own hands.

"Remember the quote you read me in that bookstore on Columbus? Writers get to taste life twice? Well if everything is only down on paper then where's your first taste?"

Jules looks at the list Christina's made and starts with the shortest on it. *Very short.* A red dot on her map; Seward Street. "We're going there today. And if there's some nice store nearby you're going to pick up something great that might inspire you."

Once they reach the little stairway, Christina bumps Jules with her hip, and asks, "You know it's not always *things* that make everything right, don't you?"

A week later, Jules has moved on to the art-filled stairways that run up and down in a dozen locations and she's lobbying that they have all day to find them.

Weeks later, by the time the sun is blocked by the canyons of tall buildings in the financial district, the pair are ready to call it a day. They make plans to come back into the city and work on the list for the stairs that they loved the most or missed going to. The city's stairways are an adventure all on their own.

Over dinner on Columbus, Jules says, "A cookbook tied to each of the stairways would be a great idea." And

Christina has to admit, it sure is.

Four months and nearly four hundred miles later, the girls are back in San Francisco. Jules wears a shirt that reads, 'I fought fog and sore feet in San Fran'. The cats they come across in an alley spark an idea and a walk of another block has Christina opening her laptop and sitting on the steps of the federal building on Battery. Firing it up, she begins making notes. First, she takes a second to label the worksheet, 'City Safari', and then gets down to it. Plans to start here, in San Francisco, then move on to other cities if it works out. It could be huge. This could be amazing. It was Jules that talked her into getting the MacBook Air. To save her wrists from all that writing.

In her mind Christina sees trading cards that are blank until the player adds a picture they've uploaded and some of their own wording. Only the tags for species and country of origin are the common denominators in this list she wants to build. Sees kids with maps to their own cities, scouring the local landscape to 'collect' animals. Live, painted, statues, posters…

A place online to post their finds. Maps with push pins saved under usernames. A way to look at other kids' maps, to compare. Make plans. Work as groups or classes with teachers. Links to rescue sites around the world. A halo on your animal card if you provide a new idea for conservation.

Maybe a splash page where animal sounds come up as the site loads. A punched ticket as a map loads when you key

in a zip code or postal code for international kids. An un-
punched ticket for cities on a list where no one has added a
map—yet.

Daily now, Christina tries asking herself 'What would
Janeway do?' She has to pull over and start making notes.
She comes up with a plan for a game. Something she can
build for the web. She's keen on the name Spell-a-Vision.
Has no idea where it came from. The ether she guesses. But
now that it's there she can't get it to be quiet.

She finds a place to eat lunch and starts writing. Jules
has gone off on some adventure of her own. And in the void
of not seeing that smiling face, Christina's mind has to come
up with her own thoughts to spend time with.

She figures it can start with a TV remote that kids can
click to move about within a suite of educational games. The
sandwich she orders is ignored while Christina lists the first
few ideas: Hangman with a teacher who's on vacation, all
dressed in beach gear and toting her towel and umbrella, her
binoculars and wicker bag, and a cell phone peeking out of
it. If the player gets a miss something on the teacher on
holiday fades away—replaced by some teacher-type gear,
maybe an audio loop of her fretful voice, crotchety, 'Oh
dear, oh dear, now *where* did I leave that?'

She makes up 15 things on the teacher's vacation
persona that can revert to full class-mode: glasses, hair back
in bun, a ruler in her hand instead of sunglasses or a drink
with a flamingo stir stick, maybe a few phone calls from the

principal, complaining that Ms. So-and-So's class isn't doing so well in spelling. Maybe the voice of other students groaning every time a player misses a guess.

God. Who needs food when you can create stuff like this all day long?

Off of Highway 101 North, as Jules pulls the van into the hostel parking lot onto Hunter Creek Road, Christina comes across her written *Win List* folded in between pages of her coastal guide. This is Klamath. The last stop on the list: False Klamath Cove and the Wilson Creek Picnic area. The DeMartin Redwood Youth Hostel.

She's had her notebook open on her knees for the last hundred plus miles; her mind's been so totally absorbed. Looking up now, she realizes that most of Jules' conversation has only been laced with the bare minimum of her, *Uh-huhs* and *yeahs*.

Christina glances around and, realizing they've arrived, promises, "Honest, I'm driving all the way back to the one, what's that, Leggett?"

But Jules smiles and wrinkles her forehead, because Christina's nose is already back to her notes, "Or not."

"What's this one about?" The two step from the van and Christina slides the side door open to grab for their bags, "I'll take that ma'am." Jules's bag hits the side of her leg as they look up at the wide two-story clapboard house, "Beautiful."

"Game six'll be, well, I'm thinking, for seashells along the coast. You know? What kind used to be in what county? Teachers could use it, even. Maybe have a list of museums.

Or a list of what native tribes lived in which areas, for how long. Like history, but *fun* history. We're in Yurok territory right now. I guess I could maybe have a few games sprinkled in."

"What about bike paths and trail heads for hiking?"

Christina stops right there, dropping her bag, flipping open the notebook. "What else?" Rooted to the spot. Dead serious. Jules laughs then looks around. Dropping her bag too, for effect, hands now on her hips. "Well, you can call it *See* Shells, S-E-E."

Christina scribbles and nods, "um-hum…"

"How about calling the Tribe pages 'Forerunners'?"

"Ancestors?"

"Okay yeah, that. And the pages for the museums can be called *U-See-ums*." Jules squats down on her haunches to stretch. Stands and brings her ankle up behind her butt. Pulling and letting out a breath. "Maybe a video page?"

"Dive Deeper." Christina scribbles. "And eels swimming in opposite directions for the back and next buttons."

"A map of the state with hot spots to jump right to the various counties. But only the ones on the coast, right?"

"Okay then, fifteen links." This is what she loves the most about Jules. Ideas fall from her brain like a string of pearls, cut loose and clattering.

"Can we go in now?"

"Sure. Gimme that bag. You must be bushed."

Over dinner, notebook still open and filled pages flipped and flipped, Christina adds more notes: a set stencil for each beach map so they'll all look uniform. A quiz on each shell and marine mammal type, murmuring, "Have them collect the items they know about. Like winning trading cards. That'll need a grid." She guesses, "More than one question for each thing?"

She still doesn't know the right words to call things. So she writes up a master list to refer to, a list of what she thinks things *should* be. Stencils, grids, key items on the grids for finding your way back through the other linked grids. Calling them buttons instead of links because that's what she sees in her mind; eels swimming in opposite directions, not navigation links. Has no idea she's been thinking in object-oriented programming. Christina—just drawing up ideas in the notebook. Sneaking up on it all.

Chapter Nineteen

A REGISTERED PACKAGE arrives on a Saturday in late
August for Char. She signs for it and walks into her
kitchen for a knife to slit it open.

Out spill three items. A cashier's check for fifty
thousand dollars made out in her name. The memo line
reads: Textbooks, living expenses + 2 more year's tuition.

The second item is a Xerox copy of a filled-in
registration form for this fall's semester at Cal State Long
Beach. Also in her name, in her own handwriting. Across the
top, stamped in red she sees: TUITION PAID. All five classes.

Char sits down hard. The blue and white mailer hangs
limp in her hands. Shaking. Her knees jangle and she feels
the rattle along her spine. She nearly misses the third item in
the package: A note. The tiniest handwriting she's ever seen,
except for once.

'A pretty wise guy once told me all any of us need are
roots and wings. Here's the second part of that… get ready

to fly. Maybe someday you'll see someone you know 'round campus.

P.S. Look into auditing for Klingon.'

Dear Reader

Thank you for reading *900 Miles*. If you enjoyed this book (or even if you didn't) please visit the site where you purchased it and write a brief review. Your feedback is important to both me and my publisher, and it will help other readers decide whether to read the book, too.

Acknowledgements

Stacy & Craig, Lynn & Tom, Mari, Althea, Alicia, and Donna & John are who brought you this novel.

I thank them all from my bottomless heart.

About the Author

E.J. Runyon lives in the US North East. Since 2002 she's found herself moving on to smaller and smaller towns, while working to become the author and writing coach she planned on being.

Her passion is focused on writing fine prose and on getting folks writing, her aim is coaching them in writing well. She participates yearly in National Novel Writing Month—an event she's been involved in since 2001.

More From This Author

A House of Light and Stone
Nominated for the 2015 Golden Crown Literary Society Dramatic Fiction Award
Swimming against the tides of her troubled family as well as her own cultural identity, Duffy struggles with the cards she has been dealt. Buoyed up by the belief of a select few, she strives to achieve the kind of self-knowledge that comes so naturally to the 'real girls' all around her. As gaps in the narrative begin to fill, and the truth surrounding Duffy's birth is unearthed, her determination to succeed is rendered all the more astounding.

Told in uncompromising clarity through the eyes of a child, *A House of Light and Stone* is at once full of heartbreak and hope, offering respites of warmth in the coldest of places.

Tell Me How To Write A Story
You might have already begun writing something you've had a great idea for. But a great story requires more than the gift of inspiration. *Tell Me How To Write A Story* takes you through the first steps of what you need to know to write well, and how to improve your editing technique.

Other Titles:
Your Little Red Book
Good People
5 Ways of Thinking to Turn Your Writing World Around

Available from all major online and offline outlets.